Crystal Clear

Nathan McWilliams

PublishAmerica
Baltimore

First printing

ISBN: 1-4241-8993-4
PUBLISHED BY PUBLISHAMERICA, LLLP
www.publishamerica.com
Baltimore

Printed in the United States of America

Part I

The lecture was really boring, Nathaniel Leonhart assumed. Here he was listening to his teacher lecture the class on how to create, augment, and disperse fireballs and lightning bolts. Nathaniel was seventeen years old, and he had already passed the advanced classes with flying colors. His personality was always unpredictable. He had a tendency to get mad over small things, and he was really impatient over irrelevant things, while staying mysteriously calm over major issues.

For this situation, however, Nathaniel wanted to shoot himself in the foot.

"Do not just ask Terra for the essence, but will it, demand of it..."

Seriously, just shut up and do us all a favor, Nathaniel grumbled to himself. He had known all too well how to use the four major elements of spells, which are fire, water, wind, and earth. And, he was already learning how to master the fifth element, which dwarfed all other elements in power and size. Besides that, he had even mastered summoning creatures.

Sometimes during this class, he would just let his mind wander; thinking about what he could do when class was over. A good idea was usually talk to his friends and try to help them with whatever problem they had.

Such a friend was Tiek. Tiek was a high-ranking archer who was half-human, half-elf. Being kin to the elves made it easier for him to cast spells, and it also gave him a naturally tall stature. He looked like a normal human, but his eyes had a brighter appearance and his ears were only so slightly pointed. But no one paid attention to that when he used his dark voice. Tiek always kept an eye out for anyone who was in danger, and his elf-like reflexes were sure to catch and kill the enemies that would threaten the life out of his friends.

"...And anymore, there are items that can magnify your caliber of magic. These items are rare, and they can assist you in casting spells," the teacher continued to drone on.

At least this piece of information did remind Nathaniel of something. He did possess a necklace that he used to amplify his power. But now, he would never have to use it again because he was already good enough to cast spells without assistance. Why, he might pawn if off and get him a nice yew battle staff! He smiled at the thought.

"Now, I want each of you to conjure a fireball," the teacher said suddenly.

Finally some action!

Nathaniel got up in front of class and, without showing off for once, created a nice fireball. Tiek was second, and he managed to create fire as well.

Emy was third. She was incredibly beautiful with a nice skin complexion and dark eyes. Emy was born after a dying sorceress renounced her powers upon Emy's mother. She was born perfectly normal, but she possessed magical talents that slightly beat out Nathaniel's powers. She was physically weak, and it was hard for her to hold her own in a sword fight.

She walked out in front of the classroom, and effortlessly created a fireball. She was awfully giggly, and smiled at her own creation. She walked to her desk and sat down. Tiek looked like he was reading his book, but was staring at Emy since he had always liked her from the time when she came to the school.

The last person was Dominique. She was a very strong knight who found herself in the wrong classroom. She constantly struggled with the classes and assignments, oftentimes making the teacher threaten to fail her. Nathaniel always thought highly of her positive attitude, and usually pondered what it was that made her suffer such bad luck. He could only hope that Dominique could pull it off.

She stood out in front of the class, highly distinguished by the armor that covered her arms, legs, body, and her back. Everybody who looked at her thought she was some big, bad, mean knightress. But to Nathaniel, she was a very nice person and he believed that nothing could hide those blue eyes of hers.

Dominique stretched out her arms and focused with every ounce of mental energy that she could tap into. Emy's eyes widened, and Nathaniel suddenly sat up straight. Both of them could feel some sort of energy form around Dominique. It was developing, but still had not taken any real shape yet.

Could she pull it off?

Nathaniel noticed a red mist emanating from her hands. He assumed that it was a fire-based attack, but his magical subconscious told him that it was lightning-based.

Suddenly, a spark had shot out from Dominique's hands and struck Nathaniel's hand. He was more surprised than hurt, making him jump out of his chair. The spell was quick like lightning, but it had burnt like fire! This did not matter, he was happy that Dominique had managed to cast a spell!

The teacher, however, felt otherwise.

"Not only did you fail to cast a fireball, but you endangered a student's life! You should be ashamed of yourself!"

Nathaniel protested immediately, "I am fine, really! I was surprised. That is all!"

"Oh, Nathaniel, do not be afraid to accuse the big mean knightress!"

"I am not a kid, and Dominique is not mean! If there is anybody mean in this class, it would be you!"

He had enough, he grabbed his things and left the classroom in a huff, but not before he asked Dominique to see him at the pier before she went to her next class.

Nathaniel had gone out and sat at the pier outside, he stared at the open horizon that was known as the Mysterious Beyond. No man, no boat, nor creature has ever explored it. Some predict that it is nothing but a large mass of freshwater. Some hope that it is not a cesspool for monstrous creatures, while others believe that it is a wonderful place with treasures that no man can imagine.

Nevertheless, Nathaniel enjoyed sitting here; letting his mind rest from the hardships he had endured in the past. He was unaware of it, but the experiences he had were taking its deadly toll on his mind. Was his anger taking a hold of his true emotions?

He had a reason for being so angry. Why else did he join this school? He wanted revenge for what his brother did to him. His name was Zèromus, and his powers were so great that they rivaled even Emy's power. Whenever a sorcerer or sorceress dies, their bodies would disappear, but their spirits would remain until they could give their powers to somebody else.

It just so happened that four powerful wizards of each specified element (fire, water, wind, and earth) gave their powers to Zèromus before they died. They had seen him as the good little boy, while they saw Nathaniel as the worst excuse of a human to ever live. After all, Nathaniel was grotesque to everybody who had seen him.

However, there was a traveling sorceress who passed the town and settled there. She enjoyed little ten-year-old Nathaniel, and she was very nice to him. She was a twenty-three-year-old elfin student who was studying the fifth element, a power that makes total mockery out of the other four elements.

Everybody saw this sorceress elf as the devil and shunned her because of this. Nathaniel, who was only ten years old at the time, could not understand why such an innocent person could be convicted of something that they could not prove.

Then, the day had come, the day of so much pain and misunderstood incompetence. Zèromus had gone haywire and corrupt. In a brilliant flash of light, the entire town had gone up in flames. Only three people died, but they were the people that Nathaniel cherished most. They were his parents and the benevolent elf.

Nathaniel cradled the dying elf in his arms, crying tears of extreme pain and sorrow. He had never had been so sad in his life. His parents' deaths were one thing, but the death of the only person who was ever nice to him? He had no friends, and it seemed like the ones who befriended him were always the ones that died. Such a traumatic event caused his personality to twist, which would leave him even more estranged.

The dying elf, that sweet and wonderful person, had given Nathaniel five gifts. First, she healed the pain caused in Nathaniel's mind preventing him from becoming detached from body and mind. Second, was the elfin knowledge of all things. Third, she granted Nathaniel the supreme knowledge of all magic. Fourth, she gave him all of her powers. Finally, she revealed her name to Nathaniel. Her name was Lilium. Such a name was sad for such a wonderful person. She slipped into a coma and died painlessly in her sleep.

When the smoke cleared, Zèromus was nowhere to be found, and the town presumed him dead. What is worse, they charged Nathaniel with four counts of murder and arson in the most serious degree. Nathaniel could not get a lawyer because they were too afraid to defend him, for they feared they would be lynched. But they admired the defense that Nathaniel prepared using the elfin knowledge he gained assisted him with this.

He started by saying that since he was not a sorcerer, he would have had to start a fire in several different places at the *same time* in order for the fire to do what it did. Unfortunately, the jury realized that he had been given powers by what they perceived as the demonic elf. Nathaniel called their bluff by saying that he had been given powers *during* the fire, but he was found guilty for arson.

The counts of murder were ridiculous. The

prosecution concocted some cock-and-bull story that he vaporized Zèromus, killed his parents, started the fire, and killed the crazy elf. Nathaniel once more proved them wrong by saying that Zèromus had disappeared, and that his parents had been killed by the fire. He also questioned them, "Why do you charge me with the murder of a person you do not even care about?"

Eventually, the whole town had seen Nathaniel as some satanic heretic and sentenced him to immediate banishment (he was too young at the time for the death sentence).

The school took him in, placing him in the standard sorcery classes. Quickly, they put him in the advanced classes, where he passed every class with high marks. Soon, his graduation would come, and he would be free to roam the world, searching for his brother, the man that had ruined his life. He swore that when he found Zèromus he would—

"Nathaniel?"

Woah! He had come to, realizing that he had zoned out deep in thought. Nathaniel even forgot that he had asked Dominique to meet him here in the pier. Dominique had seen him staring out at the Mysterious Beyond, being nothing but utterly quiet. When she got his attention, she sat down on the pier next to him, letting her feet soak in the water.

Dominique started, "The teacher told me that if I can not create a fireball by tomorrow, then I am out."

Nathaniel sighed in disgust. "That teacher needs to put a sock in it. He thinks he is so cool because his dad is the principal."

He kicked out his foot in the water, watching the water fly in the air and then come down with a splash.

"I miss the old teacher," he ended.

"Did you need me for something?" Dominique asked.

"Yes, I do. Do you remember the lecture the teacher rambled on about?"

Dominique scratched her head. She was very keen on remembering what she was told, but it took awhile to figure out what that crazy teacher was talking about.

"Oh yeah, the one about the items that amplify your powers?"

Nathaniel smiled. "Exactly, and that is what I wanted you here for."

"But they are rare, do you have one?"

"You see this necklace?"

Dominique looked down at the necklace around Nathaniel's neck. She liked the red jewel that was crested in mold, but she was too afraid to ask him about it, because she was aware of the past and corruption that Nathaniel suffered as a kid. She assumed it would make him upset if she tried to bring anything up.

"So, are you going to give that to me or...?"

Nathaniel laughed and put on a sarcastic tone. "Hey! Do not read my mind!"

He unclipped the necklace and handed it to Dominique. Very carefully, she wrapped it around her neck and clipped it. She could feel some sort of sensation at the pit of her stomach, like another arm was there. But soon, the feeling disappeared.

"Okay, that 'feeling' you might get anytime soon is what Emy and I call the third arm. With that 'arm,' you will be able to manipulate any spell you want. Everybody has a third arm, but it is more difficult to control when you are a knight or an archer."

There was a long pause.

"Well, go on, try a fireball!"

Dominique nodded; she raised her right arm and put her mind to it. She tried to "use" her invisible right arm to create the fireball that Nathaniel requested. At first, nothing happened. But then, some sort of energy began to form at her hand. It was as if she was able to "grab" the spell out of some sort of other world. With a small flash of light, there was a perfectly formed fireball at Dominique's hand.

Nathaniel smiled. The sun was about to set, and it had definitely gotten a lot darker, but the light that emanated from the fireball glowed a beautiful light, and it made Dominique look absolutely beautiful, as if she was not already.

Dominique had let the fireball go out, because if she did not start walking to her last class of the day, she would be late and therefore, penalized.

"I want to show you something cool," Nathaniel said. "Take my hand."

Naturally, Dominique was skeptical. She had heard of these stories about how the stronger wizards could teleport anywhere they wished. While it was true, and it was what Nathaniel had intended, she was sort of hesitant because this *was* Nathaniel, and he was scary looking. But then again, he did not ask to have that meritorious scar across his face.

He still had his hand out, and she grabbed it.

WHOOSH! The background around her was dissolving at a rapid rate. It looked like someone was dripping black dots all around her, and pretty soon, her entire surroundings were black, and there was absolutely no sound. She looked at Nathaniel, who did not have a single expression on his face. It was as if he was frozen in time. Dominique could still see Nathaniel's hand holding hers, but there was no feeling! No touch! *Interesting*, she thought.

Eventually, dots of color were filling the void, black areas. Those dots soon took shape and the area around her was becoming the place where she needed to be, writing class. She felt relieved that she was not going to be late for her class, but something odd had happened.

Nathaniel had vanished! He had never teleported himself with her. He had only done a singular teleportation and that was it. It would take her five minutes to walk back to where Nathaniel was standing, probably laughing his head off!

Five minutes away, at the pier, Nathaniel *was* laughing. He was happy that he had managed to help someone, who was in need, but was laughing because he knew Dominique thought that he would actually take himself with her! Oh well, so he was not able to pawn off the necklace and get something better. The yew staff would have to wait...

He smiled out at the Mysterious Beyond as the sun vanished over the water...

A few years had passed. Nathaniel had turned nineteen and had graduated from the academy. Once again, he was the only wizard in his grade, and kind of felt lonely how only a few people went to his graduation ceremony. He tried hard to disguise the scar across his face. The rest of his scars are well hidden by enchantments and spells performed by Lilium when he was ten. This was why his hometown thought he was evil, because they assumed he sold his soul to become physically appealing.

The principal was talking and congratulating Nathaniel, and he was aware of the trouble his son, one of the teachers, had with Nathaniel. The principal and Nathaniel got along very well, and sometimes teased the teacher with good and unmeaning humor. He finally ended and asked Nathaniel to give a final speech.

He rose up out of his chair, and he gave his speech. He started by saying that he was very happy to have attended such a fine school, which was usually what every other graduating student would say. Since he was the only one being honored, and most ceremonies took hours to complete, he talked about how he enjoyed the classes, enjoyed the teachers, and how his friends became an important part of his life.

Then, Nathaniel started to falter in his speech. His mouth was halfway open, but neither words nor speech came out. He then realized that *none* of his friends were at the graduation ceremony. He looked around, realizing that it was unnecessary because there were so few people.

His eyes began to water, and he dared not to speak. He knew that if he tried to talk, his emotions would win over and his voice would crack, revealing his vulnerability. He was alone, truly alone.

Speak, man!

You can do it!

He tried to will himself to speak, but no force on Terra could make him continue. The principal, a man who realized that friends were important, understood what was going wrong and quickly took over. Nathaniel was left standing there, saddled with loneliness. How could they have not attended? Tiek, Emy, or even Dominique, none of them were here. Not even after all he had done for her; she could not even attend his graduation.

His eyes caught a moving object.

What was that...?

He zeroed in on that object. He could only make out

the blond hair at first, but the sun soon gave away whom this person was. She was wearing armor, and armor shines well when it hits the sun.

Dominique?

Immediately, Nathaniel dried up the tears in his eyes and stood up abruptly, trying to determine if this person was Dominique.

Why, it was! She was running in a dead sprint to the graduation, knowing that she was very late. A heartfelt smile ran across Nathaniel's face from ear to ear, so she had not forgotten, she was just simply late. The principal was about to finish.

It did not matter anymore; he had a friend to witness his graduation...

Nathaniel had graduated, and he was gone from the school. Dominique, Tiek, and Emy were the only three left in the classroom who still took the course. Soon, they would graduate (they started when they were six years old, Nathaniel was ten, so they would graduate sooner) and would be able to explore the world, which was what Nathaniel intended to do, along with a little quest of taking down his brother.

The teacher, who still taught the same class, talked about the differences in staves when it came to the wood.

"The wood of the staff is what makes or breaks it. Trust me on this one, oak is a good wood, but compared to willow or yew, it would not stand a chance."

Tiek was writing down notes, taking all of this in. He had a bow that was made of maple, and he already knew that maple was stronger than willow and oak, but it was not stronger than yew. Yew was rather expensive, and he understood that Nathaniel had wanted one for a long time, but he was always stuck with the willow staff that he had. He could remember Nathaniel's face light up when he got his first staff made out of pine, and then Tiek's parents immediately gave him an oak staff.

"Tiek! Are you paying attention?"

"No," Tiek was honest, "sorry."

The teacher was taken aback; no one had been honest like that in his class. "Well, I appreciate your honesty, but please daydream at a different time."

The teacher continued to talk, and Tiek accidentally let his mind wander a second time. He was still a little angry that Nathaniel liked someone like Dominique. If he had it his way, he would have asked Nathaniel if he could have had that necklace. But then again, Dominique would have failed the class if it had not been for Nathaniel's help.

It did not make a difference now; he still thought Nathaniel was whipped. Seeing Emy walk up to the room and cast a spell was one thing, but watching Dominique, a simple knight, perform spells that almost compared to his, that was enough to send him into a bout of rage.

Likewise, he knew that he was sort of ill minded himself. After all, he only liked Emy because she was just gorgeous, but so did every other guy in the school.

Emy knew Tiek had liked her, and she did not jerk his chain like she did all the other people, particularly because he did not even attempt to ask her out or anything. Emy liked those blue eyes and blonde hair of his. When she first met him, she thought he was Dominique's brother because they both had bright blue eyes and blonde hair.

He needed some kind of way to prove himself! He wanted to be a hero, not waste away in this school! He wished that some villain, any villain, would just burst in the classroom and declare a challenge!

He should not have thought too soon, because the windows in the classroom had suddenly shattered, hitting the teacher in the eyes and blinding him. Two gigantic men—one in red armor, one in blue armor—had slowly walked in the room, each one with a smirk on their faces.

The person in the red armor was Agnes. He was a huge red knight who joined leagues with Zèromus when he was given the offer. All of his life, he trained and honed his sword fighting skills to the point where he would get worse if he continued to train. Zèromus knew he would be perfect for missions to come. His armor was impervious to all physical attacks made against him. He was practically a walking tank.

The person in the blue armor was Rubdra. He was a gigantic archer who, like Agnes, joined leagues with Zèromus when given the offer. He and Agnes were brothers, and while his brother spent his time with his swordplay, he took the liberty of learning the archery skills. He became so advanced that his skills would wane if he were to train more. Rubdra was impervious to all magical attacks and arrows. He was, like his twin brother, a walking tank.

"We found her! This is Emy!" Agnes shouted, his voice deep like those of demons.

"Uh...yeah," was the response from his brother; his voice too, was also demonic.

At first, no one said anything, because they were a little dumbfounded over what was happening. First, some big, and obviously stupid guys, burst in the room. Then, claim they are looking for someone as unimportant as Emy!

"Let's take her!" Rubdra yelled.

"NEVER!" Tiek cried out in his loudest voice. He jumped into the air, and threw a knife at Rubdra and launched a fireball at Agnes. Both projectiles hit their mark, and Agnes was sent flying while Rubdra groaned as the knife hit him in the knee.

Tiek landed, poised, and ready to protect Emy. It seemed kind of corny, because now his efforts to not try and impress Emy were wasted. Oh well, a woman's life is more important than a man's.

Dominique stood up and immediately ran after Agnes, unaware that he was immune to blades. She drew out her sword and aimed for his head, only to have it deflected. Agnes brought up a fist and punched her hard in the stomach, picked her up and launched her across the room, hitting the wall.

Agnes's moment of glory was short-lived as Tiek came from nowhere and somersault kicked Agnes across the face. He once more was sent flying. Immediately, Rubdra had gotten up and held a dagger across Tiek's neck, but Tiek was quick enough to elbow him in the place where it hurt most. Rubdra hit the ground groaning.

"TIEK!"

Agnes, who was careful this time to keep Tiek in his sight, had grabbed Emy. Tiek cursed to himself as he witnessed this, these guys can recover quickly! But it did not matter now. Tiek had lost, he had given his best to protect Emy, but his efforts were in vain, and Dominique was lying lifeless on the floor. The teacher was blinded, so he could not help.

Then, someone had tapped Agnes on the shoulder and he turned around. At first, he thought he saw Zèromus, but the scar across the face told him it was someone else.

"Uh-oh..."

It was Nathaniel, but...his skin was dark purple, his eyes were bright red and his hair was white. His robes were royal armor; this was the evil side of Nathaniel.

Nathaniel had firestorms for fiery eyes. He lifted his hands and Agnes was floating helplessly in the air. Like a rag doll, he flung Agnes across the room, hitting the walls, the cement floor, and the ceiling. He would have "let go" of Agnes and let him fall to the ground, but he slammed him down violently.

Rubdra was on his feet, in awe that some sorcerer that had access to dark powers had just defeated his brother. He was more strategic than Agnes, and he considered that he might win if he fought from a distance, because he was immune to magic, no matter how powerful Nathaniel's spells might be. He was wondering why Nathaniel would not just charge and attack him, was he asking for a death wish?

Rubdra took out his crossbow and loaded it. He pointed at Nathaniel's head, who did not think it was necessary to move.

He fired, and if everything had gone correctly, that bolt should have pierced through Nathaniel's skull, killing him instantly.

But how could he explain the bolt just inches from Nathaniel's forehead, floating in midair? The bolt then turned around and pointed at Rubdra, Nathaniel fired it psychically.

There was blood on the ground. Rubdra was quick to raise his hands in natural reflex. The bolt had hit Rubdra's armor, but it still went through and stuck out the other side of his hand. Since he had not been hurt like this in the longest time, he had a suppressed cry of pain. He quickly recovered and ran away.

Agnes also got up quickly and tried to run away, but Nathaniel simply shot out his arm and Agnes was once more dangling helplessly. Nathaniel brought him closer and held him upside down, face to face.

"What did you want from us?" Nathaniel asked. His voice was not human. It sounded like a demon's voice mixed in with Nathaniel's own voice; it was like listening to two distinct voices that each said the same thing at the same time.

"It was not me that gave the order!" Agnes whimpered.

"Then tell me who your master is!" The demon voice in Nathaniel grew more prevalent.

"It was Zèromus! It was your brother!" Agnes was whimpering.

"And what did he want?" One voice was purely Nathaniel's; the other voice was the one who had the darker tone.

"He wanted Emy, because he is on a quest to absorb every sorceress' powers so he can defeat you!"

"What do you mean?" The voice was halfway mixed.

"With the fifth element, you are more powerful than Zèromus can actually dream of. He can not absorb a sorcerer's powers unless it was willingly given to him!"

The confessions were true. Nathaniel knew how to absorb a sorcerer's power, but not a sorceress', unless it was given willingly (such an incident was when Lilium gave him her powers).

"Who is the next target?"

Agnes was shrieking. "Hildegard! The Queen of Vicksber!"

Nathaniel flung Agnes out of the schoolroom and he wound up landing on his brother Rubdra, who had still been running away from Nathaniel. This news of Zèromus seeking Hildegard was important indeed.

Hildegard was one of the most beautiful women in

Terra. Like Emy, when she was born, she possessed a magical power that was so great that Nathaniel would have a hard time with her in a duel unless he tapped into his evil power. Hildegard could make any man besides Nathaniel swoon with unforgettable lust, and they constantly asked for her hand in marriage.

Nathaniel was unaffected because he at one time liked Hildegard, but she was gracious enough to cast a spell that caused him to "get over it." They did not get along, but they had their own lives and problems to live out, but with Zèromus pursuing her now, Hildegard was going to have a bigger problem.

Nathaniel looked out at Tiek, Emy, and Dominique. Immediately, he saw that he was still in his "evil" state. He quickly changed out of it, with his eyes, skin, hair, and armor turning back into the way it was.

"What was that?" Emy asked, wide-eyed and curious.

"To tell the truth, I am not quite so sure myself," Nathaniel responded.

He walked over to Dominique, who was still a little winded from her injury.

"I missed you," he said to her. Tiek rolled his eyes in the air, trying hard not to laugh.

"What are you going to do?" Dominique asked.

"I am going to go to Hildegard and warn her," Nathaniel answered.

Nathaniel set off to Vicksber and bid farewell to his friends again. Soon, his vengeance would be settled and he would be able to live a perfect life with no problems or any nightmares haunting him.

Then, his mind stumbled upon a flashback.

"Nathaniel, do you get along with your brother?" Lilium asked.

"No, he always picks on me and Mom and Dad will not make him stop," Nathaniel said, his voice was higher pitched and more childish.

Lilium giggled. "What would you do if you were as strong as him?"

"I would show him who is boss!"

Lilium smiled, but then her face showed signs of sadness. "That path is difficult to traverse."

"Why?"

"You are too young to realize, but revenge is like a poison. If you let it take over you, then you will only become as bad as the person that you are trying to kill."

Nathaniel's eyes were blank with confusion.

"I can sense great evil in your intentions, and I can sympathize with you, but you must have control over it, or you will become something that you will never be able to handle."

"Why are you telling me this?"

"Because vengeance is a great sin and sins can never be forgiven if you use it as your drive, your will that carries you on. Of course, the people could forgive you, but could you ever forgive yourself?"

Nathaniel was still walking while he was remembering this. Lilium was right; vengeance would get in his way from living a normal life. He knew he did not the heart to kill anyone, and he believed that when his parents and Lilium died, it was by accident rather than purpose. But still, Zèromus deserved to be punished, because he still did evil deeds. With the newfound power that Nathaniel had, he would be sure to put it to good use.

This power that Nathaniel possessed was a lower form of the fifth element. It "unlocked" a hidden potential that feeds off of evil thoughts, desires, and deeds. While Nathaniel had tried to be good all of his life, he had trouble keeping his thoughts and wants to himself. What is more, the vengeance that he sought caused his evil form to be extremely powerful. He also realized that since he unlocked this new potential, there's someone...or something, else in his mind that had some influence in his actions.

This thing in his mind could be compared to the angel on the left shoulder and the devil on the right, always trying to boss you around and telling you what you should do.

Nathaniel kept walking, and he just about within city limits when an arrow landed by his foot. He looked up, and saw three bandits around him, each one holding a sword.

"Ah!" Nathaniel laughed. "Some practice!"

The bandits said nothing, one of them had a look of anger, but he was taught by his masters to not let a victim's threats get to him. All three of them charged at Nathaniel, but then they were suddenly hanging in midair. Nathaniel did not want to hurt these guys, they did not know any better.

He was having fun making play toys out of these bandits. He suddenly noticed that his grip on one of the bandits was failing, and soon one of the other bandits started to touch solid ground. His hands were shaking, his thoughts flickering, what the hell was going on?

There was darkness of shadows within his mind, and Nathaniel put his hands up to his head, something was controlling him, but what was it? He had to fight, or else something bad would surely happen!

The last bandit was put back on the ground, now realizing that Nathaniel was having trouble controlling himself. He was standing there, moving around violently, looking like he was trying to shake off someone that was clung to his back or something. *That is his loss*, the bandit thought; *he is dead meat now.*

They charged one last time when Nathaniel exploded in malicious shadows. It knocked back the three bandits once more, this time confused over what Nathaniel was doing. Was he just playing tricks on them, or was he really this messed up?

When the shadows dissipated, they saw Nathaniel, but in his evil form. He glared at one of the bandits and the thief was screaming as he was lifted in midair and then a great eruption of red liquid spouted from his chest. The mess hit the other two bandits, who were now panicking over what had just happened.

They made a run for it, and then they were stopped in their tracks, immobilized and unable to move. Nathaniel appeared in front of them, smiling sinisterly. He looked at one of the bandits, and he just exploded in a mass of blood and body parts. The last bandit, knowing he was going to die, was shouting for help. Nathaniel reached out his hand and touched the bandit on the head.

He started to walk away, and the bandit was being engulfed in a black liquid that was taking over his entire body. In a matter of seconds, the bandit was covered from head to toe in this black goo, and then it melted in a puddle. To put it in Layman's terms, Nathaniel turned this bandit into a puddle of goo.

Nathaniel started to shake and quiver at sudden speeds. Soon, his body had a split, half of it was the true Nathaniel, and the other half was the evil form.

"Why did you do that!?" Nathaniel demanded.

"Because they were attacking you!" was the response.

"Ultimus, I could have taken them down myself, WITHOUT your help!"

"When will you realize that mercy is for the weak? Do you remember why you enlisted my help?" the voice said.

"I never enlisted! Lilium gave me these powers, and as me being the owner of these powers, you have to do what I want."

"How about a deal?" the voice asked.

"Ha! You just want to make a deal so you can break it!" Nathaniel crowed.

"Seriously, I will do what you want me to do, only if you agree to kill your attackers! If you say yes, I will kindly be patient until you need my help. I will even let you spare a few people!"

Nathaniel thought about it for a second. He knew that Ultimus would try to find a way to go around this deal. But, he had to think about what good it would bring. If he agreed to this, he would not have to worry about Ultimus taking over him. But he knew that if he agreed to this, he would have to kill every person that had intent to kill him, unless they were special to Nathaniel.

An eye for an eye, fair enough.

"Agreed!"

Nathaniel had control over himself again, fully aware of what he just did. At first, he was glad to get Ultimus, the spirit that controlled the evil form, off of his case, but he was also sort of worried about it. Ultimus was not totally evil, but he had a deep desire to kill, maybe all he wanted was to have at least some sort of say.

Nathaniel put his thoughts aside and continued on to the town of Vicksber.

Vicksber was a city that was actually above ground, enchanted by many unbreakable spells that kept it floating above the ground. The reason why it floated was because it was hovering above a swamp that had water so poisonous that it would devour the unfortunate victims that would fall in the swamp.

But the citizens of Vicksber had nothing to worry. There was absolutely no way to break the spells that held the city above the swamp. Also, there hasn't been a death caused by the swamp in years, and the government was not responsible for deaths caused. After all, they were endangering themselves by *living* there.

Nathaniel immediately entered the city gates and headed southward. He was passing by the merchants that had interesting things to sell. He knew that he needed to get to Hildegard and let her know about the impeding dangers that lied ahead.

"Get your magical staffs! I only have one yew staff on hand, get it while it is still fresh from the last yew tree on Terra right now!"

Immediately, Nathaniel found himself in this certain tent. He looked at the yew staff; it was splendid in design and definitely powerful. He asked for the price.

"It will be 10,000 gold crowns, are you interested?"

10,000 gold crowns! Prices like that, and he would be able to afford to buy a house! He started to wonder if giving away his necklace to Dominique was beginning to show its worth.

He continued to walk on to the palace, which was a sight to behold. Most palaces were made of iron, sometimes bronze. This castle was made of mythril, a metal that proved to be resilient to steel and iron.

The royal gates opened for him. They knew Nathaniel was a well-respected sorcerer in terms of magic. Hildegard, as powerful as she was, probably sensed him walking towards the castle anyway.

The inside of the palace was just as magnificent as

the outside of it. Hildegard was truly a queen of fashion with great tastes in decoration and style, who else could have carefully designed a room with such elegant drapes, paintings, and décor? Furthermore, there was a marble statue of Hildegard in the middle of the main room! To add to it, the statue had almost every detail of her face and body! The eyes, the angel face, and the well-shaped physique, all had been perfectly sized, scaled, and sculpted.

Of course, the statue was a far cry from how Hildegard actually looked in person. She was not conceited or anything similar to that, but she was a bit touchy on how things and events would approach. One time, she hanged a palace guard because he stood too close to her.

Nathaniel kept walking to the grand hall where Queen Hildegard reigned. As he walked closer, he could recognize Hildegard, and the smile that sent him the warm greeting that he was more than welcome here. He approached Hildegard and bowed his head down lower than her fluffy, white robes, which draped along the floor.

Hildegard could have raised her scepter and granted Nathaniel permission to rise. But instead she *literally* picked Nathaniel up and gave him a hug. The music that was playing in the background suddenly went abrupt, because the composer was hired to play songs that related to Hildegard's mood. He had never seen the queen so happy.

That was it, some happy, emotion-feeling music. He raised his hands and the violins played a very wonderful tone.

"Where have you been?" Hildegard and Nathaniel did not generally get along, but that did not mean that they spent the rest of their lives as enemies. It simply meant that one could get too much of someone else and be driven mad.

"I've been roaming the world," Nathaniel said. He did not want to stay and chat like normal people. He wanted to get the word out that her life was in danger and that he wanted to protect her.

Then, he might ask if he could stay.

Hildegard took the floor again. "How about you stay and share some stories?"

Nathaniel was reluctant. "I would but I need to tell you something important first."

After an hour of chatting, Nathaniel realized that he still hadn't told Hildegard of the dangers that lie ahead. He was sitting in a comfortable chair, but he was brooding over how Hildegard was *still* speaking to him about some glass slippers that some housemaid dropped.

"Would you like to join me in a swim?"

Nathaniel's eyes were red, "No, I REALLY need to speak to you about something important."

After what seemed like an eternity in the swimming pool, and with Hildegard showing off her graceful dives, Nathaniel soon realized why he and Hildegard did not get along in the first place, she talked way too much. If he had any sense, he would interrupt Hildegard and state what he needed to say.

"Well, I feel refreshed," Hildegard said as she was putting her robes back on. "Would you care to join me for dinner in a few minutes?"

Nathaniel once again declined, and he found himself staring down the face of a fish at the dining table. He was also given a bottle of sherry, a really strong substance that could incapacitate him if he was not careful. He was highly opposed to alcohol.

He was soon tired and depleted of energy.

Hildegard had managed to prevent him for three hours from telling her of the dangers that laid ahead for her. After talking, swimming, and dining with the Queen, he finally put down the glass of sherry and broke into a rage.

"I've had enough! I can not take it anymore!"

Hildegard was startled. "What? Is something wrong?"

Nathaniel was flustered. "I just can not believe how I've been trying for hours now to tell you that your life is in jeopardy!"

Hildegard covered her face with her hand, and she realized why Nathaniel had been so stressed. She felt stupid and dumbstruck. On the other hand, deep down she was glad inside that he had just blurted it out. Such an act could get a person hanged. Instead, Nathaniel cared for her as a friend to the point where he couldn't care if he died for something like interrupting the Queen.

During the next few minutes of explaining, Nathaniel had filled Hildegard in on the details, such as who Zèromus was, what he was capable of, why he was stripping sorceresses of their powers, and what could happen to Hildegard if he were left unchecked.

"What could he do to me?" Hildegard asked.

"Knowing Zèromus, he could take advantage of you, but I am not entirely sure if he is interested in women or not. If he does not find a use for you, and if he takes away all of your powers, he could just kill you where you stand, hoping to cause political turmoil within Vicksber to create war."

Hildegard got lost at the part where Nathaniel said, "Take advantage of you."

Nathaniel had about thrown his hands in the air. He was thinking about leaving Hildegard defenseless and letting Zèromus take her powers and anything else he might want from her.

Without surprise, he noticed that the palace guards had all faced Hildegard, aiming their crossbows at her.

Nathaniel was about to attack, then realized that he was paralyzed where he stood. There was an assassin who managed to get around his sight and disable him.

Hildegard shot out her arm, and an invisible force sent the guards flying off of their feet. She was about to reach Nathaniel to aid him until a figure appeared out of the air and clutched her throat.

Who was this? This person looked like Nathaniel, minus all the scars and battle wounds. Rather, this look-alike appeared more attractive and suave. His eyes were bright blue and his hair was silvery blonde. He was wearing an outfit of the most opaque of all colors. He was wearing plate armor that was colored black. He could have been compared to a black knight in a bedtime story.

Nathaniel recognized him as Zèromus, and he had Hildegard where he wanted her. He knew that once Zèromus stole Hildegard's powers, his strength would be equal to that of his own twin.

In a matter of seconds, Hildegard began to feel weaker and weaker as her incredible powers were being siphoned off. She could feel her strength waning and the pain was gaining strength. Nathaniel could see her ribs and other bones show up. What was happening was Zèromus had been taking in Hildegard's powers so fast that her muscles were contracting, and gave the appearance that she had been starved to death.

Hildegard had trouble breathing. Her contracting

muscles prevented her lungs from working properly. Her heart, stomach, and all other organs also had trouble functioning. The only thing she could do was bear her teeth at the culprit.

Zèromus had taken every last drop of magical power from Hildegard and released her. Her muscles expanded back to normal and covered her bones. She stood around for a few seconds; her head hurting because of the blood rush. She felt like every body part had cramped up. She knew she had to recover, because now that she was no longer powerful, Zèromus could take her out easily.

Nathaniel knew that Hildegard was still physically powerful. She had a thin build, but that allowed her to move faster than many other people.

She rose up her fists and was ready to fight Zèromus with her bare hands.

Zèromus was dumbfounded. He knew he could kill Hildegard with a simple magic spell. He knew he could fiddle with her heartbeat and kill her instantly. He also knew that he could tamper with her body and make her explode in a mess of body parts, similar to the same way Nathaniel killed one of the attacking bandits.

Unbeknownst to Nathaniel, Zèromus followed a code. If someone had the nerve to fight him with their fists, then they did not deserve to die unfairly. Of course, he would kill them eventually, but at least they would die with some sort of honorable dialogue in their obituary, such as "She was brave enough to fight Zèromus with her bare hands."

Zèromus raised his hand and the palace guards walked away. He also drew out his weapon. It was a sword with a blade that was about five feet long. It was lightweight, and with it, he could reach a long way and hit someone.

He started the fight with a lunge, and Hildegard dodged to the side, the blade slicing inches from where her face was. She jumped into the air and threw three daggers. Zèromus managed to dodge two of the daggers, but one of them hit his plate armor and deflected, causing no damage whatsoever.

Hildegard landed and reached within close proximity. She was skilled in fist fighting and managed to hit the unprotected parts of Zèromus' body. While it did not hurt him much, he was getting more frustrated that he could not strike her; she was simply too fast for him.

Zèromus then tried to punch her, but Hildegard managed to get her last shot on him, when she reversed the punch, spun around, and struck his nose with the heel of her foot. It did not matter how powerful a person was, a broken nose was always painful.

Nathaniel knew this because Hildegard did the same thing to him a long time ago.

Zèromus got up slowly. In terms of magic, he would have won, but physically, he just got his rear end handed back to him.

Hildegard jumped into the air again, but Zèromus grabbed her white robe, which dangled in midair, and slammed her back to the ground, where the floor cracked upon impact.

She was lying on her back, which had obviously broken from the brunt. She couldn't move at all anymore, and she knew that her death would come quickly.

Zèromus appeared and put one foot on Hildegard's stomach. Without hesitating, he thrust the mighty sword in Hildegard's stomach, and slowly pushed it down. It also passed through the floor and into the earth. Hildegard's body made some sort of gurgling sound, and then she coughed blood and fainted.

"NOOO!" Nathaniel was thrashing around, even in his state of paralysis. He knew Hildegard was still alive, but only for a few seconds, and then she would die from organ shutdown.

Zèromus disappeared along with his sword, and Nathaniel was struggling step by step to reach Hildegard. In his state of paralysis, moving was a pain in the rear, and it became a war to keep his balance.

Two more steps, Nathaniel's legs almost quit on him.

One more step, come on, you can do it!

There!

He made it to Hildegard, who was looking at him with half-closed eyes. It was ironic that he fell, his hand just barely touching her hand. It did not matter, that was all he needed.

Blue sparks shot out of Nathaniel's arm and made its way to Hildegard. He had performed a healing spell. What a healing spell did was immediately find its way to the most serious of injuries and restore it. In this case, it was Hildegard's stomach and her shattered back.

The spell repaired her internal organs, made the gash vanish, and enervated her exhaustion. The spell also fixed her back. She sat upright, and stood up, realizing that Nathaniel just saved her life.

But for some odd reason, she felt really light. It was as if she lost fifty pounds. She figured out that she had no more magical power. She couldn't even do the simplest thing as lifting something up with her mind and putting it down gently.

She turned around, and Nathaniel was gone! Where did he go? She looked down and there he was, still in paralysis.

Paralysis is almost like playing freeze tag. When you are paralyzed, you are "frozen" and you need to wait for someone, either enemy or ally, to "tag" you again so you can move once more. This is why paralysis is useless in wars and battles, because there are so many people around touching you.

When Nathaniel was cured of paralysis, he stood up and studied Hildegard; her eyes still blue as ever. She still had the smile that he enjoyed to look at. But now, he needed to head towards Ginnorum, where the last queen could be in danger of losing her powers.

"Nathaniel..."

Nathaniel turned around, and Hildegard was crying! Why? She was alive, what was she sad about?

Hildegard was born with an insurmountable amount of magical power. It was what made her what she was, an all-powerful queen. With the loss of her powers, she was suffering from a harsh reality check. But Nathaniel knew that Hildegard had a wonderful personality and she did not need power to be a nice person.

He put his arm around her shoulder and sat her down on her throne.

"No matter what happens, or what the people say, I still think of you as a queen."

He bowed down to Hildegard, lower than her robes.

He rose up and crossed his arms.

"Take care," he said as he disappeared. Hildegard sat there, with her hands in her face. The composer, and his musical group, who had been hiding during the attack, came out and played a sad song reflecting Hildegard's confusion and sadness.

Nathaniel could only teleport himself or other people to places that he had already been. He had visited Ginnorum numerous times, and it easily became his favorite city to go visit. The queen was one of his friends, and in Nathaniel's opinion, her powers were slightly stronger than Hildegard's, and since she was older, she had everything covered in the beauty department. Her name was Britania, and she was the most powerful sorceress in the land as of now.

While he was teleporting, his thoughts shifted around Dominique. How was she? What was she doing? Did she think of him?

What the heck was he thinking? Of course she did not. She would only think of him when he was around her. What's more, she probably thought he was weird, but would not admit it. It was odd though; he would talk to her in person and could notice a few things about her facial expressions that would tell him that she simply did not think of him the same way he thought of her.

"You know, sometimes it is best to let go."

Ultimus was right; there was no point in liking someone who did not share the same feelings.

"She is just another person to you." Maybe Dominique is not just another person, but she really did not need to take up all of Nathaniel's thinking time.

"She does not deserve all the time you devote to—"

"Alright! Will you shut up?!" Nathaniel realized that Ultimus was just trying to help him, but he wanted to be selfish for a while. He never had a girlfriend in his life. Yet, in his school, he would look around and notice a girl with a ring on her finger (symbolizing companionship). He was constantly told, "Oh, you will find someone."

Surely, when you have been told that for nineteen

years, it drives you nuts to the point where you could think of a girl and pray to God that she liked you back, only to find out that you are prayers had fallen on deaf ears.

It felt like jumping off a cliff and hoping that you could fly.

Well, Nathaniel smiled to himself; he *could* fly, if he ever needed to. But technically, it felt like that.

Back at the school, Tiek, Emy, and Dominique were in the classroom where the teacher put some time aside to talk about Nathaniel. Their graduation would come within a few days, and they could go and do what they wanted to do in life.

"You know, Nathaniel was always hyper," the teacher said. "He would always get jumpy and excited over things that did not seem important. Yet, he would always find something good about it."

"Yeah, I remember how he and I would always have some kind of magical duel," Emy remarked.

"I just know he did not always make the right decisions," Tiek added.

Dominique was silent...

"Well?" Emy nudged her.

"I do not know. I just know he liked me. He is a really nice person, but sometimes I think that he takes situations on with a primitive mind, like a child's. There were some things where Nathaniel would think it over and come out shining. But sometimes, he would just explode in frustration. It is as if he punishes himself for being a failure."

Emy sighed. "Very true, I learned the hard way how to approach him whenever he was angry."

Tiek was amused. "Oh, and how do you approach him?"

"Well, I learned that when he was angry, you just

do not suddenly *approach* him. He is the kind of person that wants people to be around him, but does not want to talk to them. What I did was stand around him until he asked if he could talk to me. It is kind of odd of Nathaniel, because here you are trying to talk to him, and then he *asks* you if you could talk to him."

"He was always polite...sometimes," the teacher remarked.

Emy continued as if the teacher said nothing, "But you know what? That is what made Nathaniel who he is. I think he is born out of his timeline. You look around and you have people in the cities that say very inappropriate things and they speak in slang that only the lower class can understand," she had strong distaste for those with "accents," "and here you have a guy who makes an effort to speak clearly and properly. Do you remember the realm of Earth? If he were born around the 1500s of that time, he would probably fit right in."

Tiek was laughing.

He took the floor. "I would not worry about Nathaniel getting hurt. You have to remember, he is a very powerful sorcerer. Sometimes, I wonder how he got all of that power. His parents were not sorcerers, neither were his ancestors. They were nothing but common people."

Dominique answered, "He told me a long time ago that a dying sorceress gave him her powers. He would always remark about how powerful she was, because she knew how to channel and use the fifth element. But, he was angry because of what his brother did to him."

If Dominique had known Lilium's name, she would have said it.

Emy raised an eyebrow. "Are you talking about that scar?"

Dominique nodded. "Yes, but there are many more scars. Some of them I think are self-inflicted, because he knew that one sorceress very well, and the loss of his only friend at that time caused him to lose hope."

Tiek was confused. "Did Nathaniel say anything about this sorceress studying the fifth element?"

"He said that the sorceress was trying to unlock the final parts of the spell. He also brought up that the first parts could only be unlocked by the emotion of anger and hatred. But to unlock the final parts, you have to have a strong focus on what you really want."

There was silence.

Emy broke it. "So what does he really want?"

"He wants to kill his twin brother, the man that hired those two knights to abduct you. His name was Zero-ma-call-it. I have not heard it in a while."

The teacher was listening in on it. "You know, murder is not illegal in this world if you have a duel, but if you kill in the city or even out in the countryside, you are tried for treason. In Nathaniel's case, he is signing his own death warrant if he finds his brother and kills him."

"I know," Dominique said. "But what I admire about him is that if something happens on the way of his little quest, he will abandon his mission to help or fix the situation."

"It sounds like you can not quite make up your mind if you like him or not." Emy giggled.

"Oh, Emy, how could you say that?!" Dominique yelled abruptly. She punched Emy in the stomach in a playful way.

Tiek chuckled. "You know, Nathaniel's quite a character. I am just glad he is on our side."

Nathaniel was nearing the end of his teleportation. Another thought was floating in his mind. He knew that Britania had to be protected, but he also did not want to spend all of his time in the castle. He also remembered the two assassins that Zèromus sent to take Emy. Nathaniel wondered if he ever had to cross paths with them again.

Ultimus wanted to kill. Nathaniel silently promised that if he met Agnes or Rubdra, he would let Ultimus do the dirty work.

At the town of Ginnorum, a guard was pacing the stone walkway of the northern entrance to the city. His primary job was to keep watch on the castle and report to neighboring cities if it was ever under attack. His name was Graf, and he had heard news that a powerful sorcerer had stolen the neighboring queen's powers, making Hildegard just a common mortal.

He did not want to worry about it. Britania was very well protected. All of her knights had anti-magical armor that would stop even the doomsday spell. Not only that, all of their weapons were augmented and modified so that any person they hit with their weapons would immediately be brought down.

Suddenly, there was a quick flash of light. When it was gone, Nathaniel appeared where the flash had originated from. Graf had his weapon drawn out, ready to strike.

Nathaniel saw Graf, smiled, and said, "Watch where you point that toy stick of yours."

Graf lowered his weapon, since it was only Nathaniel. "You need to quit using that teleporting spell so close to me; you know it scares me all the time."

"I will try to remember that. May I speak to the queen?"

"I am sorry. I would let you in, but she is busy. She is working on matters within Vicksber, concerning Queen Hildegard. She already knows of the threat, and expected you would come. But, she did not want you to visit her."

"Okay, are there any missions I could do for you?"

When Nathaniel met Graf, he had seen that the guard always had some sort of problem that needed to be fixed. When Nathaniel graduated, he found a steady source of income doing odd jobs for Graf.

"Yes, actually, I want you to do some criminal hunting around here. It seems that a few vagabonds have caused a lot of trouble in the town streets. Their numbers are few, but they are a bit stronger than some of the countryside bandits that you are used to."

"Alright." Nathaniel nodded his head.

"If you manage to find the leader, you need to dispose of him, but all the other thieves can be put in the jail cells. Please do not kill them, just kill the leader if you can find him."

Nathaniel rolled his eyes. "Alright, fine."

"The thieves can be found in alleyways," Graf said. This was something that sounded really obvious, and could only classify as common sense to anyone.

Of course, if Nathaniel lacked anything socially, it was the ability to use common sense.

Ginnorum was a huge city. It was big enough to the point where you could get lost in there. But this was Nathaniel's town; he knew it inside and out, particularly because it was his favorite city. He enjoyed walking the alleyways and the corners. Originally, he took walks in the town to take down thieves and criminals, because he could easily take them on.

It was time for some bandit hunting.

After about an hour of walking around, he still had not found anything. Wow, he thought, these criminals were not your average run-of-the-mill wrongdoers. He knew that he could have found them easily if they were normal bandits, but this was a challenge!

Let's see, Nathaniel observed. He already looked ahead, that was obvious. He looked around his left and right and even looked up sometimes.

Oh crap...He did not look behind.

WHAM!

Nathaniel found himself face down on the ground. The bandits had been following him for the past hour, probably laughing over how he couldn't find them.

Well, they had their laugh, because now Nathaniel was going to have his.

Nathaniel got up and brushed himself off, staff in hand. In a matter of seconds, six bandits surrounded him. Each of them had a mask that concealed their faces, and a headband on their forehead. Nathaniel also looked at their weapons; each of them had a large number of kunai (*throwing knives*) on hand.

He groaned. No wonder why he could not find them, they were half bandit, half ninja.

Nathaniel wanted to have some sort of fun with these bandits. Of course, if he found the leader, he would have to kill him. He decided to let Ultimus have his way with the leader.

"Alright, which one of you has the pleasure of getting their butts handed back to him first?" Nathaniel taunted.

The first hybrid bandit threw six kunai at Nathaniel. They were sharp as claws, but Nathaniel could easily stop them in midair, turn them around, and fire them back at the target the same way he reversed Rubdra's crossbow bolt.

The opponent, who had been cornered against the

wall, soon saw his own weapon being fired against him.

He quickly dodged the kunai from hitting him.

It was a good thing actually. Nathaniel remembered that he was only supposed to kill the leader, and leave the common ones alone.

Using his psychic powers, he lifted the enemy and flung him off of the battlefield. (On the battlefield, this is known as being "Ejected.") With that, there was one down, five to go. Nathaniel then put his hands together and a strange green light was surrounding him.

Besides the fifth element unlocking Ultimus, it also unlocked an array of spells that Nathaniel could use to his advantage. With a green flame in his hands, he puffed it in and blew it out at the bandit-ninjas, sending two of them packing.

There were three left, and Nathaniel had one last idea.

Nathaniel's hands had yellow sparks coming out of them; he slammed both of his hands down on the ground and a huge wolf came out of nowhere. Nathaniel mastered the art of summoning creatures a long time ago, and the more he summoned a creature, the stronger it would be. He found his war wolf (whom he called "Pooch") to be a friendly helper.

"Hungry?" he asked Pooch.

Pooch had its tongue out, panting heavily.

"Go fetch!" Nathaniel pointed at the remaining opponents, and Pooch growled and snarled. With dust in the air, it was chasing the three remaining ninjas. Eventually, Pooch could only go so far and then disappear like a shadow, but the ninjas would not notice until it was too late.

That left the leader, who, Nathaniel believed, was standing behind him.

Of course, he was. The leader looked no different from the rest, except maybe the obvious appearance that he was taller. There was something about him that looked different from the others; he looked as if he had the upper hand from the very beginning.

The leader did a back flip and performed some weird gesture. Suddenly, he and Nathaniel were trapped in a whirling wall of fire. Nathaniel realized from this that the leader had a proficient power in field spells.

Field spells were unbreakable. There would be two people in a field, and it would go down when one person or the other were dead. In Nathaniel's case, he had to kill the leader, or else he would never escape the wall of fire.

It was time to call the cavalry. He holstered his staff and took a battle stance. The leader could see an eerie light form around Nathaniel. Soon, there were shadows exploding all around him, as if he were performing a kamikaze spell. After all the lingering darkness cleared, the leader was looking at a person who looked similar to Nathaniel, only with purple skin, red eyes, white hair, royal armor, and a sword that seemed to sing the Hymn of Death itself.

"Hell calls for you, scum!" Ultimus roared. He drew out his sword and made a single slice that seemed to cut the wind. The leader stood there, already dead without even knowing it. After seconds of silence, the leader's body was falling to the ground in thousands of nicely even pieces.

Light exploded from Ultimus, and Nathaniel was back to normal. Soon, the fire ring died down as if someone had sprinkled water over it.

Nathaniel's job had been completed. He started to walk back to the castle, where Graf would give him an honest day's pay. There were townspeople around him, staring at this hero who got rid of these would-be criminals.

He felt exposed almost as if he did not really deserve the attention. The opponents were not really that hard anyway.

Eventually, after what seemed an eternity to escape the many people staring at him, he managed to get back to the castle, where Graf held a bag of platinum crowns. This was different, Nathaniel mused, and platinum crowns were worth one hundred gold crowns. He hoped that there would be one hundred and fifty in there, one hundred so he could get that yew staff, fifty so he could enjoy a week of not doing odd jobs.

Nathaniel tried to start small talk with Graf. "Do you know of anything special today?"

Graf scratched his head for a second, and then his face lit up as if he worked hard to get this information.

"Why yes, there is a graduation going on at the school of wizardry."

"What!?" Nathaniel suddenly got mad and picked up Graf.

"Hey! Do not kill the messenger! You will make it on time if you teleport…"

In a blinding flash of light, Nathaniel was gone once more.

"Or at least," Graf continued. "I think you might be a little late. That is not a problem, is it?" he asked, knowing Nathaniel couldn't hear what he said.

Back at the school, there were three people standing on the stage. One could be recognized by his bow and blonde hair, the other could be pointed out for her shining armor and blue eyes, and the last could be distinguished by her very nice complexion and black hair. These were Tiek, Dominique, and Emy. Soon, they would be out of the school, and able to live their own lives.

Well, at least Dominique would, because Tiek and Emy felt like they were going to die because they were not sitting together. They finally started going out and they were both happy. Unfortunately, the school was aware of this and decided to separate them during the graduation.

The principal stood out and gave a speech saying how wonderful it was to have these three kids in their school. In honesty, the principal had a feeling of sadness about him. There weren't any more teenage kids (these three people were seventeen) in the school, and the oldest group of kids that were left was the nine-year-old kids. Age was getting to him, and it was sad to know that sorcery was becoming unpopular, with all the new inventions that replaced magical aids.

Maybe something would cause the popularity of magic to turn around one day.

Dominique was happy that she was finally graduating, but something was missing. Where was the person that helped her all of this time? Where did he go? She put her head down.

She was not crying, but it would be wrong to dismiss the feeling of sadness within her. Nathaniel was not going to show up to her graduation, which was enough to make her feel miserable.

Dominique could not quite understand, although she could jump to a few conclusions. Nathaniel was probably still hell-bent on finding and killing his twin brother, Zèromus. She could not figure out how he could have so much malice against his brother, but it would have been nice if he had put aside his quest and take the time to be at her graduation.

It is not that she liked him or anything, far from it. She never liked Nathaniel, not at all. She would wonder sometimes if she was being too nice to him, if that was the reason for him liking her. She could not just blame him all the way, because she knew that he was lonely and heartsick. Dominique just sincerely wanted Nathaniel to come to her graduation, because they were friends, and friends would do anything for each other.

She looked up, and a figure with red robes and a scar on his face waved at her.

Suddenly, a feeling of peace settled within Dominique, as if all was well with the world.

The graduation was over, and Dominique saw Nathaniel about to leave. With all deliberate speed, she ran over to Nathaniel and hugged him. Nathaniel, at first, was dumbstruck because he had just turned around and before he knew it, someone clung to him the same way a child would cling to its mother.

"Do not go yet. Could we talk a little or...?" Dominique couldn't finish the sentence.

Nathaniel, who had not wrapped his arms around her, was dead silent. He had never had anyone ask him to have a conversation.

"It is just one question...and then...and then you can go do what you need to do," Dominique said.

"Alright..." Nathaniel replied.

"What are you going to do after you are done with...you know, Zèro?"

"Zèromus?" Nathaniel replied as if it were not a big deal. "When I get done with him, I am going to...well, perhaps I could show you."

Nathaniel held out his hand. Dominique, even after all this, still hesitated to grab his hand. That answered some of Nathaniel's questions that he was too afraid to ask. Dominique *still* did not trust Nathaniel.

If she did not trust him, then she did not deserve to know what he wanted.

He lowered his hand just when she was about to grab it. Dominique's face suddenly went white, had he lost his patience with her?

Nathaniel's expressions showed disappointment along with a little disbelief. He started to glow with a light. "I will be seeing you sometime." With that, he disappeared.

Dominique was left standing there, still with her hand out, touching nothing but the air around her. There were serious gaps that needed to be filled one day. But how would she fill them? That was probably one of the hardest questions she ever asked herself.

Why did she care so much!? That question was enough to drive her nuts!

Nathaniel was in the vortex, teleporting to Ginnorum again. He almost had a tear running down his face. Ultimus could be heard cackling.

"Nathaniel, Nathaniel, Nathaniel. I told you she did not care."

"Have you ever...cared about someone?"

Ultimus answered seriously, "You know, there were a few in my life, but they did not like me as much I would have wanted them to. Why do you like Dominique so much?"

"I do not know anymore, and I hope I do not find out."

"You need to toughen up. That much is for sure. I know you are hurting, I can feel your pain almost. I am not saying I could relate to it, but I could probably be in your shoes and not do any better."

Nathaniel chuckled. "You never used to talk like this, am I getting on your good side?"

Ultimus laughed. "Hey, I could be a nice guy, if given the chance."

"Hey, Nathaniel!" Graf yelled. "Just *who* are you talking to?"

Nathaniel snapped in surprise. He had finished teleporting and gave the appearance that he was talking to himself. Nobody could hear Ultimus talk unless he was in evil form.

"Umm...I was not talking to anybody. Sorry."

"Well, Nathaniel, the queen would like to see you!" Graf exclaimed. He seemed merry and cheerful about something. Although he did not tell why, nothing seemed to hide the expression on his face that signified happiness and satisfaction. He tapped on the door and it opened with a rumble. Graf then motioned his hand towards the door, gesturing Nathaniel to walk in.

Nathaniel did so, and the moment he walked through, he was within ten feet of the magnificent Queen Britania. In awe, he turned around and could see the door that he was supposed to be a few seconds from. He turned around again and was blinded by Britania's pearl-like smile.

My goodness, Nathaniel thought, *she is still a sight to behold.* Neither simple nor advanced words could describe this beauty. The only thing that could be safely assumed was that Britania was practically a walking picture. She had dark brown eyes, a very fine tan, and a very anatomically correct body. She was not too muscular, neither too flimsy. Britania was the ultimate example of the ideal woman.

Nathaniel, at one time in his life, could think of nothing but Britania. Thankfully, he let maturity force him out of it over a long period of time. If there was one thing that threw him off, it was her personality. She did make an effort to be nice to everyone, but there were occasions where Nathaniel would slip up and receive a harsh ridicule.

But, that was in his childhood, and both he and Britania grew up together. They were separated when she had to take responsibilities as queen, and she was born from a bloodline of all-powerful sorceresses, making her the most powerful sorceress of her time.

He was going to walk towards her, but then a strange pain entangled his leg and forced him on his knee. Britania suddenly went from happiness to worry. She told Nathaniel numerous times in the past to not bow down to her in the past. She knew that Nathaniel would not bow unless he was told. Here, it looked like Nathaniel was struggling to stay standing.

Nathaniel was surprised and confused, because he did not know what was going on.

"She...killed them all..." It was Ultimus' voice, and it seemed to be from the depths of *his* soul.

Britania immediately rose from her well decorated chair and rushed towards Nathaniel, but when she got close enough, there were shadows coming from within Nathaniel. The shadows were different. They actually howled in pain and roared in anger. Britania stayed put.

"My family is gone because of that conceited wench. I must have revenge!" Ultimus yelled.

Nathaniel was in extreme pain. He felt like his whole body was burning to a crisp. If he resisted Ultimus taking control, it was painful. If he did not, it would not hurt. He was trying to fight off Ultimus because he was looking like a fool in front of Britania.

"You must let me out! I must destroy the dragon!"

"I do not understand!" Nathaniel cried out as his eyes were turning into a fiery red.

Ultimus had a reason for acting so belligerent when he saw Britania. Ultimus, at some time in his life, was an elf that lived prosperously in the Ab'Dornum. However, his days were nearly cut short when a gigantic brown dragon came and destroyed his hometown.

He would have died, had not his sister saved him. She knew how important Ultimus would be in the future, so they both combined their powers, causing Ultimus to disappear within his sister.

The sister elf fled to a town where everybody seemed to despise her. Even with all of the kind acts she would perform, the people simply did not like her. She spent most of her days in her cottage, trying to figure out how to separate herself from Ultimus.

Of course, to do that, she must be able to use the fifth element.

She could use it, of course, because Ultimus was able to use it. The problem was that she was female. Females were simply not able to use the fifth element. Britania or Hildegard could not even pull it off if they wanted to. The only reason she could use it was because she and Ultimus had combined powers.

Then she met a young ten-year-old boy. He was a boy who hated his twin brother, who constantly tortured and tormented him. The boy had scars everywhere on his body, caused by the twin brother. The kind elf performed spells that concealed the scars, and it was by the boy's request that the scar on his face be kept visible, as a reminder of what he had been through.

The next day, she awoke to the sound of an

explosion. In a matter of minutes, the entire town was on fire.

She walked out of her cottage and there was a sorcerer with silvery blonde hair and bright blue eyes staring right at her. She could sense evil power coming from him, and he was only ten years old. After a furious firefight, it was the elf that was defeated. The assassin flew away, leaving her to die.

After what seemed like an eternity, a young boy held her up. He was crying softly, but at least the elf would not die alone. With a wink, she transferred all of her power and knowledge to the boy. Before she did so, she spoke to Ultimus one last time through telepathy.

"Ultimus, please be patient and good to the young lad. I can see that he will become something legendary one day."

"But, sister, he is nothing but a common boy! It would take him fifty years to master the fifth element!"

The young woman smiled. "He will master everything five times faster than everyone else. He may not have powers, but his talent is very impressive. It was as if he was made for this kind of thing."

Ultimus wondered, "How will he feel about my voice in his head?"

"He will not have to. You just have to stay quiet until he learned some of the fifth element spells, and then say that you were released or something and that he has to cooperate with you."

There was silence for what seemed like forever.

"Very well, I promise to be nice to the boy, and I promise to kill the dragon that destroyed our hometown, and the man who took your life."

"Take care, Ultimus," the woman said, moments before her final breath.

"Farewell...Lilium."

For the next nine years, Ultimus stayed silent and observed the way the boy, called Nathaniel, lived. When he was twelve years old, he went to the school. Lilium was right; Nathaniel showed great promise in magical power and knowledge. It was not because of her extra powers that gave Nathaniel the boost either. He did magic as if he were made to do it, he was just unfortunate that he was born without any powers of any kind.

The people Nathaniel was around with had interested Ultimus. At first, Nathaniel took a liking for Emy because she was good looking. Eventually, Nathaniel wised up and began to take a liking for Dominique. Ultimus had to endure a lot of talking that the two exchanged between each other. He did, however, have a high interest in Tiek, because he was half-elfin.

This brought a new way of thinking about Ultimus. Nine years earlier, he and his race held all sorts of hostility towards the human race. Elves did not look very much different from humans, except the pointed ears. Ultimus did look much like Nathaniel in his true form. A normal elf did not have purple skin; this was just what would appear because of the transformations.

When Ultimus saw Tiek, it more or less told him that the elves and the humans could now co-exist together. He knew he had to put aside his differences.

But now, it did not matter if Britania was human or not. He was going to have his revenge on her. The hair, skin, eyes, and armor, all had changed to Ultimus, and Britania was staring a similar appearance to Nathaniel. Both he and Nathaniel had the same exact power level, but there was something that made Ultimus deadlier, more prone to be scared of.

She could not quite place it, but her best guess told her that it was simply the looks that made him appear scarier. Or perhaps it was the rage within Ultimus that carried him to do what he wanted.

Ultimus drew out his sword and pointed it at Britania.

"I am going to destroy you!"

He charged, unknowing and uncaring of the consequences that could lie ahead. Nathaniel, having no control (except for the amount of power he could give Ultimus) over himself could only watch in terror. Nathaniel had his own powers, and so did Ultimus. Because Nathaniel was not going to let Ultimus use any of his powers, it was going to be difficult for Ultimus to take down Britania.

Britania had not fought a foe for a long time. The last time she fought, she morphed into the dragon to destroy the town of Ab'Dornum. That was nine years ago, when she was twelve years old. While she was rusty, she was still very powerful, and she was very nimble, too.

Ultimus brought down the sword upon Britania and missed, but the impact of the sword hitting the ground caused the marble to crack in all directions.

Britania did a quick teleport from behind. While she was in midair, she brought up her leg and was about to heel drop Ultimus. Of course, Ultimus teleported and she brought her foot down upon the marble, cracking it some more. That frustrated her, she was much stronger, faster, and smarter than Ultimus, but could not get a hit on him.

During that split second of frustration, Ultimus came from nowhere and thrust his knee into Britania's back, crushing and snapping her vertebrae. She flew into one of the pillars of the gigantic room, and she fell lifelessly with a thud.

Ultimus thought he had won, but he was wrong. Britania stood right up and both Ultimus and Nathaniel could see the bones on her back. They were misshaped, out of place, and looked as if it would take years to repair. But, to Ultimus' amazement, the bones snapped, popped, crunched, and connected their way back together. Britania was on her knees, trying to get up. She had not been hit like that in her life. Although her body could heal itself, the exhaustion it gives could leave her helpless soon.

The transformed Nathaniel snarled in frustration. He charged again at Britania, but Britania was then surrounded by a spherical shield, knocking Ultimus back. Ultimus raised his hands and the shield shattered like a broken glass. Britania was still on the floor, trying to recover from the shock of the initial hit.

But Britania was on the floor for a reason. Ultimus got close enough, and Britania whipped her body around like a lash and spin kicked Ultimus, sending him flying through the air, stopped only by the wall. He fell down gracefully on the floor, but he slowly got up, as if he was never hurt.

What happened was that when Nathaniel was himself, Ultimus would share the pain and damage, when Ultimus' health was critical, Nathaniel would suffer the full pain. When Ultimus came out, it was the other way around. The blow took out about half of Nathaniel's health, but it had brought confusion among Britania, Ultimus should have been critically injured.

Regaining his battle stance, Ultimus took a final charge at her. When he got closer, he teleported behind Britania and was going to bring his sword down once more. Britania, however, was wary of this and performed a back kick, striking Ultimus in the stomach, and sending him flying through the air.

Ultimus smiled, this was what he wanted. He wanted Nathaniel's energy to go low enough so he could be allowed to use his powers. When either person's energy was low, Nathaniel's body would automatically allow any use of powers to keep it alive.

With the surge of new energy, he instantly recovered midair.

"I hope you should know that Nathaniel is literally hurting for you!"

This disturbed Britania. She finally realized that all the damage she had done was dealt to Nathaniel and not to Ultimus. With the sudden demoralization, she tried to defend herself from the onslaught of attacks that Ultimus dealt. While she blocked every single punch, swing kick, roundhouse kick, and uppercut, she could feel the fatigue just eating at her.

There were not very many weaknesses that Britania possessed. But she could have sworn that when one was exploited, it was used without the aggressor's knowledge that it was a weakness. What was bothering her was that she had dealt a lot of damage, but all of it was diverted to Nathaniel.

Ultimus was about to shoot an enormous fireball at Britania, but then a few spouts of light exploded from him, and Britania was looking at Nathaniel for a split second.

"Do not be afraid! If you hit him now, he will definitely feel it!"

Then Ultimus took him over again with a growl. The words from Nathaniel brought new strength to Britania. With confidence, she charged up all of her magical powers. Ultimus was going to charge towards her, but then stopped when he saw the warm glow around her. Feeling threatened, he fired a gigantic icicle at Britania.

The icicle should have pierced through Britania, rupture her stomach, go through her back, and kill her. But the icicle just melted upon contact and the water on her had disappeared as if her body were a sponge. Britania was taking in all the power she could. What she was hoping to do was hit Ultimus hard enough so Nathaniel could take over, and then everybody could breathe a sigh of relief.

It was risky, because if Britania was overcharged, the extra power would surely kill Nathaniel. If it were undercharged, the excess of what would not be used would damage Britania to the point where she would be left vulnerable.

With the energy that was gathered, she held out her hand a bright ball of light formed in her palm. Over time, it grew a little bigger, and it eventually became the size of a gigantic bounce ball.

Ultimus snarled. He did not know what Britania was up to. All of the elfin knowledge he had could not tell him what spell this was. All he knew was that if the ball hit him, it would probably knock him out, allowing Nathaniel to take over.

Britania spun around and launched the ball, hitting Ultimus square in the chest. With great force, he was knocked off of his feet and blown backward, slowing down only when he rammed into the pillar. Unfortunately, the force was great enough to knock the pillar down and Ultimus was stopped only the already crumbling wall.

Ultimus started to shake and spasm at sudden speeds. Within seconds, Nathaniel emerged from within. The spell had worked wonderfully. He was sitting with his legs spread out and awry, his face riddled with gashes, and blood was everywhere. Nathaniel couldn't complain though, because at least he had control over himself again, and Ultimus right now was knocked out.

Britania ran to Nathaniel and gently approached him. He was really hurting. She kneeled on one knee and touched his face with her hand. Nathaniel would have said something to compliment Britania, but right now, he did not want to say anything.

She began to sing in a foreign language. Nathaniel knew it was in elfin, and he also knew that Britania had such a beautiful voice. Everything about her was beautiful; it was as if she was meant to be so perfect. But Nathaniel knew better than to pursue her. He simply did not hold that feeling that every other man would have. They lived, laughed, and fought as friends, and they were happy and content that way.

Over time, Nathaniel's wounds disappeared, and he was able to stand on his own. He looked upward and stood up, and then he took a look at the person that healed him. Instead of seeing a sullen face, which was what he expected, it was a happy face, a face that expressed gratification, and it was simply cheerful.

But then Nathaniel looked down, and there was a long, red, blade sticking out of her stomach. She fell down on her knees for the last time, and fell to the ground. As she fell, Nathaniel could see a face that also had a smile. The figure had silvery blonde hair, bright blue eyes, and a face similar to Nathaniel's.

It was Zèromus, and he came in while Britania was

fighting Ultimus and stayed hidden until she was left unchecked. He could not take her powers, because she used too much of it fighting Ultimus.

Nathaniel fell with Britania and held her up for the last moments.

"I love you," she said, meaning it like a friend.

"I love you too," he said, and then Britania died.

Nathaniel stood up, staring at his twin brother. He drew out his battle staff and blacked out...

Nathaniel awoke from the blackout, and he was in a bed surrounded by all of his friends: Dominique, Hildegard, Tiek, Emy, and Graf.

"We did not think you would wake up," Tiek said casually.

Nathaniel started to freak out. The only thing he could remember was drawing out his weapon and racing towards Zèromus, and then he could remember no more. Emy and Dominique were both holding him down as he started to go into a rage. Then, realizing that Ultimus could use this opportunity to repossess him because of his rage, he started to calm down.

"What happened? How am I still alive?" Nathaniel asked, confused, scared, and searching for any and all answers.

Emy knelt down beside him and answered as best as she could.

"That Zèromus character that you always talk about? You two had a magical duel and you made quite a ruckus out of the castle. You fought him, and you had him pretty much beat. You were going to lay down the final blow, but then you started talking to yourself, like you did not even want to kill him. After about thirty seconds, you sealed Zèromus in some sort of coffin and told him that he would be gone forever.

"That is when Dominique came, and she saw you beating yourself up. Believe me; you were going to kill yourself if she did not stop you. You are lucky that a staff is made from trees and not iron! She actually manhandled you to the ground and knocked you in the head, rendering you unconscious."

Nathaniel then asked, "What about Britania?"

Graf looked as if he was going to answer, but then his voice cracked, and his face welled with tears. Being a guard of the queen, he was not allowed to cry, show feelings of emotion, or feel sympathy for someone else. But, those rules did not have to be followed if certain conditions were met. He started crying and he left the room.

Emy bit her lower lip, and then she put her arm on Nathaniel, hoping that he would take the news well.

"Britania is gone..."

Those simple, small, and unmeaning words had cut into Nathaniel's heart far better than a hot knife going through butter would have done. With those words, Nathaniel realized that one more of his friends were gone. With those words, he knew he could not talk to her in person, laugh with her, sympathize with her, cry with her, or be angry at her again.

Nathaniel stared off into the space. Dominique, Emy, Tiek, and Hildegard all watched him silently mourn his best friend's death. He stood up out of his bed, paced the floor, and had his hands behind his head. During all of this, tears were gushing up and his face had swollen slightly, turning into a red color.

"Did I...did I miss...her funeral...?" he asked, unable to get the words out.

Dominique nodded her head.

That action only made Nathaniel feel worse. He headed towards the door and walked quickly out.

The moment he walked out that door, the people inside that building could hear a bloodcurdling yell that lasted for an eternity. All the while, the ground started to shake vivaciously, and the people had a hard time balancing themselves.

Dominique tripped and looked out the window, what was once a bright afternoon turned dark and stormy. Nathaniel's anger was so great that it caused the very light of the day to turn into the grimmest of all darkness. What could he do when he put his mind to it?

Then a guilty thought struck her mind, what would he do if *she* had died?

When Nathaniel left that building, nobody heard from him. He did not leave any kind of note or information telling anyone where he would be. It was like he had disappeared, never to be heard from again. Dominique and Emy both thought that he would be back within a few days, but a few months had passed, and they started to worry about him.

Those months progressed to a year. When that happened, Zèromus' henchmen, Agnes and Rubdra, attacked and took over the town of Vicksber. Without Hildegard's magical power, the city went down without a fight. While it was not confirmed if Zèromus was there or not, Agnes and Rubdra both made it quite obvious who they were fighting for.

Of course, the cities of Ginnorum, Parlona, and Kazastrat could have rallied their armies and crushed the army that took hold of Vicksber, but the magical conclave decided to not take any action until further notice.

"These political figures are idiots," Tiek sighed with disgust as he let the newsletter drop to the ground. Emy came in the room, sat beside him, and put her head to his chest.

"Why are you so uptight, dear?" Emy asked.

"I just get so sick of hearing these leaders saying that they will strive to any and all ends to preserve peace, when they know quite well that if they do not act, Terra will tumble into another war."

Emy seemed to not care. "Maybe it will all blow over like the last time."

Tiek sighed. "But the last time that happened, we actually *did* something about it."

"By the way, have you heard from Nathaniel?"

Tiek covered his face with his eyes. How many times did people ask him that question? Why could they not figure out that he seriously did not know anything about Nathaniel's whereabouts? Every time his name was mentioned, he always remembered the time when Nathaniel left that building and caused the day to turn into night, all by the power of his magic alone, and not with the assistance of Ultimus.

"I do not know, as always."

"Well, I hope that he is okay, because it would be bad if we went into war and did not have Nathaniel to help us."

Tiek sighed again. "I am not so sure if he is alive. It is not that I lost hope in Nathaniel. It is just the way he stormed out of that building, in a horrifying rage. I looked in the papers hoping to read something about him. I actually hoped that he would destroy a city or something so I could track him down and try to talk to him. But, he really did disappear."

Emy raised her head and looked at Tiek, and then she lowered her head on his chest again.

"If Dominique were ever in trouble, Nathaniel would come for her, I know it."

Dominique worked as an officer in King Ginnery's army. King Ginnery was the prince who replaced Britania upon her death, and he actually turned out to be a natural for raising an army. He quickly took into the account that Dominique was able to cast magic because she possessed a rare necklace that allowed her to cast medium level magic. Not only that, he was impressed by Dominique's physical strength (and he had a small crush on her looks).

Dominique would spend every day showing cadets and soldiers how to handle a sword, and the proper footwork needed to take down an opponent. She had a small unit of her own, consisting of fifty soldiers. When that was done, she would spend an hour each day sharpening her sword. She loved thinking about how the blade would help her reach her goals, how it would help her achieve what she wanted. But to do that, she must keep sharpening her blade.

Her sword was actually a pretty well made sword. It was half-Golem toothed, half-diamond, making it an extremely sharp sword. It used to be double edged, but she customized it to where the back end of the sword could be used to knock someone out rather than kill the victim.

Dominique stopped sharpening her sword and she stared off for a while. It had been a year since Nathaniel went up and disappeared. She was aware of the hard times that were coming, with Vicksber being taken over and the threat of the war spreading to Ginnorum.

She was also aware that if Nathaniel had been here at this time, none of the events would have happened. She could not say that she was dying to meet him, but it would have been nice if she heard something about him. It would not have mattered if he was heard about the next day dying by rat poison; it still would have been a relief to know that he was alive all this time.

Dominique picked up the sharpener and picked up her sword. She was about to use the sharpener, but then she threw the object down and gritted her nicely even teeth.

"Why do I stand here and think about it? I know very well that I can easily go out there and look for him!"

Oh goodness, I just talked to myself, she thought.

She was right though; she could do something about it, rather than wait for another year and not hear anything from him. It was not that she liked him or anything; it was that she wanted to know how he was, and if he was still alive.

She grabbed fifty parchments, and with her pen, wrote the following message.

> *Dear comrades!*
> Your commander wishes you to the Ginnorum castle as soon as you receive this letter. Keep your heads high and your eyes open, because we are going on a manhunt. Of course, because of the hard times approaching, please pack your armor and weapons and do pack for a month's travel!
>
> Your commander,
> *Dominique Delacroix*

Dominique had re-read the letter and had her messenger send it to the fifty locations where her knights resided in. She could not believe what she was doing. She was going to send fifty of her knights to every location of the world, looking for the sorcerer that gained the reputation as to "Turn the light into darkness."

Why was she doing this? It did not make sense. Did she love him? No.

Did she care for him?

Surprisingly, and to herself, she nodded her head...

Part II

"I know what I want to be when I grow up!" twelve-year-old Nathaniel cheered.

"And what is that?" the teacher asked him.

"I want to be a all powerful sorcerer!"

The teacher laughed. "Well, if you want to be an all powerful sorcerer, you will have to learn to say 'an' before a word that begins with a vowel!"

Nathaniel stared at the teacher in disbelief. "When were you my English teacher?"

The teacher, who was reading a report on Nathaniel, did not raise his head, but he did look up at him. "Well, I am not your English teacher, but I do strive to help everyone to speak properly! Hey, you are only twelve years old, you can not do everything now. But when you get older, maybe one day, you could be an all powerful sorcerer."

The teacher chuckled over what he had said and continued reading the lengthy report. It was saying that Nathaniel possessed an extreme amount of magical power. While most of the energy was latent, the energy that was potent could be enough to make him graduate early. It was also saying that he murdered four people: his parents, his twin brother, and an elfin lady who was pronounced a devil in that hometown.

He lowered his arm, which was holding the report, and could see Nathaniel smile at him. He did not look like the kind of person who could murder somebody.

"Nathaniel, could you cast a fireball at me please?" he asked Nathaniel.

Nathaniel was excited; he was going to do his best to show the teacher what he got. He jumped up on the table and spread his arms out.

Then he hesitated. "How strong of a fireball?" he asked the teacher.

The teacher thought for a second, then he grabbed a piece of paper and said, "The biggest one you can possibly do. If you can knock me off my feet, you will get a B. If it can push me out of this school, you will get an A."

"Alright, here I go!" Nathaniel busted. He spread his arms out again, and began channeling all of his energy.

There was a girl sitting next to Nathaniel at the time. She was two years younger than him, making her ten years old. She was also very energetic, eager to learn how to cast magic. The only problem was that she was destined to be a knight. Her parents were knights, their parents were knights, and their entire lineage consisted of knights. Nevertheless, she strived to try to cast magical spells.

She sat next to Nathaniel so he could help her with all the assignments that the teacher left for them.

She stared in amazement how Nathaniel made spells look so easy. She could see Nathaniel moving his hands around, watching the fireball get bigger and bigger. Eventually, it had the diameter of a hoolah hoop. The teacher started to back away until the wall stopped him. This may be a little too much.

The school was built of high quality wood, maple. In

these times, mythril had been discovered and iron was soon becoming the norm for building structures. With magic, sorcerers could shape the iron and make anything they wanted out of it. A person from the realm of Earth would state that Terra was a medieval setting with some modern aspects to it.

To Nathaniel, magic was modern...

He fired the sphere of pyro at the teacher, who regretted asking Nathaniel to do so. He was knocked off of his feet and the force of him flying through the air destroyed the wall. He flew for a few yards before finally touching the ground. Blue sparks erupted from his hand and went to the paper that he had been holding. Although it was somewhat burnt, it was still usable.

The sparks embedded itself onto the paper, and formed the single letter: A.

Nathaniel smiled. He was only twelve years old and did not understand how much damage he did to the school building's wall. The principal walked by and looked at the wall that had a massive hole through it. He also noted Nathaniel standing on top of the desk.

Before jumping to conclusions, he found his son, the teacher, on the ground. The teacher looked at his father, gave a thumbs-up, and talked as smoke puffed out of his mouth. "He passed!"

The principal beamed towards Nathaniel, shook his hand, and walked out smiling. Now, they had a reason for explaining to the board why they needed an iron made building!

Nathaniel looked down at Dominique, who was wide-eyed at the magnitude of such a fireball. She was also surprised that he hit the teacher without getting in trouble! Even though the teacher asked for Nathaniel to hit him, it was still humorous how Nathaniel managed to get the teacher like that and get away with it!

He said something to her, but she did not quite hear it.

"What?" she asked, holding her hand up to her ear.
"I like you!" he answered, a little loudly, to be heard by the other students in the classroom.

Dominique laughed to the memory as she was on her horse in the Kazastrat Mountains. She had made up her mind days ago to search for Nathaniel, who disappeared after the late Queen Britania's death. Before he left and disappeared for a year, he released a magical rage so powerful that it caused the daytime to turn into night. This gave Nathaniel a worldwide recognition.

Dominique did not go on the search alone. She came with the accompaniment of fifty soldiers. Each soldier was trained in all aspects from one-on-one fights to full field fights. Besides that, each knight brought his squires, thinking it would be a great way to train them, and to give them a little experience before they went to knighthood.

Each knight brought five squires, making the entire search party two hundred and fifty-one. There were two and fifty hundred men, and one woman. Dominique split up the entire search party to go to parts of the world and search for the fabled sorcerer Nathaniel. There were ten teams of twenty-five (five knights, twenty squires), each team searching everywhere.

Dominique did not have to fear the knights getting in danger. They were each armed to the teeth, ready to take an army. The armor they were wearing was anti-magical armor. Anti-magical armor was a pain in the rear to construct, because it took a blacksmith three years to make a full set of armor that could reflect magical spells.

Even after all the effort it took, Anti-magical armor could only defend so much. While it significantly lowered the amount of damage from a magical spell, it was not perfect. It couldn't block fifth element spells and it doesn't work at all while it is raining. With fifty anti-magical armors out there, that was one hundred and fifty years worth of effort.

Before she left on the quest to search for Nathaniel, she talked with Emy and Tiek about the whole matter. Emy was optimistic, claiming that the moment she was in trouble, Nathaniel would run to her rescue.

Tiek had thought otherwise. He believed that Nathaniel had been long since dead. He told her it would be nice if she could return the body, so they could give it a burial and such.

Dead or alive, it did not matter to Dominique; she just wanted to see him again, even if he was unable to speak to her because of the grip of death. She continued to traverse the mountainside of Kazastrat. Dominique believed that the altitude could be where Nathaniel wanted to seek solitude and silence. It seemed to be the ideal place, since there was a freshwater river flowing from the summit and there were trees everywhere that bared lots of fruit.

At first, she did not find anything, but then she found a cave entrance. It was still a good distance up, but she had all sorts of hope that Nathaniel could still be residing there, if he resided there to begin with. The altitude from the mountains was causing her breathing to become difficult and heart to pulse a lot faster than she would have cared for. Normally, she was used to hiking around in the mountains, but after jogging a long distance, fatigue caught up to her.

She stood still for a while, trying to get her breathing to slow down and her heart rate to stop pulsing like a jackhammer. As she was taking the quick break, a plethora of thoughts ruminated throughout her mind. Why did Nathaniel have to run off like that? He did not even give a warning or hint. He simply left, and that was it.

Nathaniel, Dominique thought to herself, *I swear, you are a real handful.*

Dominique started to breathe at a normal rate again. She was glad that she thought ahead and told her knights to wait for her at the bottom of the mountains, particularly because she did not know if altitude affected horses or not (and the last thing she needed were sick horses). With her breathing normal and her heart rate at an average pace, she continued to hike for the cave entrance.

She was about there when she saw a plant on the ground. Immediately, she recognized it as the emerald leaf. These leaves were common, but hard to obtain, because they were so high up in the mountains. Merchants sold them in Ginnorum and Parlona, but they charged ridiculous prices for the leaves. They were useful on the battlefield, because these leaves, when placed on a wound, would cause the gash, opening, or any status ailment to simply disappear. It was a good substitute for a sorcerer's healing spell.

She plucked the leaf from the ground (these leaves grew on the ground) and put it in her bag. Once more, she continued up the mountain. She was very close to the entrance, and she believed that Nathaniel was there. Even if he was not, she could probably ask the inhabitant if they had seen Nathaniel.

Finally, she was there. The entrance did not lead to a cave. She could tell by looking at the walls that a sorcerer had shot at the mountain and crafted a small room for shelter. Dominique walked in, and was staring at a crude interior room. It had a makeshift bed in the corner, a fire pit in the middle, and lots of potions. She noticed that there was a bag of shining dust on the bed. She could tell immediately that it was bag of black magic. People who couldn't use magical spells usually used a bag of black magic.

Dominique could use magic. She had a necklace around her neck that amplified her powers. Most knights couldn't use magic at all, and Dominique happened to be one of the gifted few that had slight powers. Nathaniel, three years ago, gave Dominique the necklace. He had used it before, but since he did not need it anymore, gave it to Dominique. Whenever she felt lonely or in despair, she would clutch the necklace with her hand, and then everything was all right. It was as if she had a hand on her shoulder to see her through.

Dominique was confused when she saw the bag of dust. She assumed that Nathaniel was here at one time and either left to get food or left to live somewhere else. Even if he was here in this cave, why did he have a bag of black magic with him? Had he lost his powers? Did he think that magic was no longer important to him?

No, Nathaniel would never give up his powers, not if Zèromus was still alive.

There was the sound of footsteps...

"Who goes there!?" Dominique snatched her sword in hand and her position in battle formation. She ran her fingers through her blonde hair, flinging it back. She had forgotten to tie it into a ponytail. That could hinder her battle performance if her hair got in the way.

The sound got louder, and soon a dark figure ran after Dominique. The figure was wearing a black cloak, keeping the identity a secret. It was a small person, but that made her fast. Dominique was quick to realize that this was not a friendly person. In a split second, she used the figure's momentum and flung the opponent at the wall.

The opponent got up, but the mask had fallen off. It revealed a very attractive girl, eighteen years old, and the same age as Dominique. She had blue eyes, brown hair, and a small build. The female ran towards Dominique and released a barrage of spinning kicks and somersault combos. Dominique could do nothing but block the attacks that kept coming. This person was extremely fast, and did not seem to be exhausted.

The opponent was just about to do another somersault until Dominique found an opening. The opponent was wearing a female archer's outfit, showing her stomach. Archers generally did not have any defense when it came to physical fighting, there defenses were more focused for magical attacks.

Dominique took advantage and punched the female square in the belly. Finally, the opponent stopped and clutched her stomach, unable to breathe. Dominique then slammed the girl against the wall, where she fell with a thud.

Surprisingly, the archer quickly got up and dove for the bag of dust. Dominique was going to stop her, but the archer was too quick. She had breathed in most of the dust and electricity bounced on her fingers. With a smirk, she threw a gigantic lightning spell at Dominique, and she could feel the pain as it paid her no mercy. Her anti-magical armor could only protect her to a point, and then it lost its defensive properties.

Dominique had purple electricity pounding her

body mercilessly. She had been shocked before, but never at a constant rate. Before long, her brain would shut down and she would pass out. She had to stop the current!

She struggled to get up and tried to walk to her opponent, but Dominique's legs betrayed her, and refused to obey. The enemy stopped the current, and Dominique was too weak. She couldn't fight if she wanted to. She fell on her back with a thud.

Nathaniel...Where is my hero?

"Say good night," the opponent said. The last thing Dominique saw was a foot aimed for her face.

Good night...

In an unknown location, a place far away where no one could walk to, a man was tossing and turning in his sleep. He found it close to impossible to get a full night's sleep. He would constantly have that nightmare about his friend dying. The worst part of it was that it was his fault.

His name was Nathaniel...

He became distant, despondent, and very moody after his friend's death. Right now, he was having a dream that Britania was talking to him. But like all of his other dreams, there would be a sword that would pierce through her stomach and kill her, but this dream was a little different.

Nathaniel, I have already forgiven you. It is all up to you to forgive yourself.

No...what did she mean? Was she trying to tell Nathaniel to not feel at fault for her death?

Think about it, there are people out there who care for you, although you may not have seen it already. The least you can do is aid them, be with them, care for them, and love them.

What was that supposed to mean?

Dominique worries about you, and if you do not go to her, you will never be able to talk with her again.

Then Nathaniel could see himself. He had a serious look on his face, and his fist was raised in the air. There was green light exploding all around him, and it soon became white. The power that erupted from within him was enormous, and it made him one hundred times powerful.

What do you really want? Is it truly revenge that you seek? Could it be forgiveness? Or could it be the quest of love?

What?

Aww, how sweet. You are in love with Dominique!

No, I am not! Shut up!

You can do it; you can do the impossible...

Nathaniel awoke in a cold sweat. His breathing was rapid, and his sheets were wet from all the sweat. He leaped out of his bed and started to get his things ready. Ultimus also awoke. He was the spiritual being that was transferred to Nathaniel when he was ten years old. At first, Nathaniel thought that he was "another voice in my head" but it turned out to be Lilium's sister.

"Nathaniel, is something bothering you?" Ultimus asked.

"I can not live in solitude, Ultimus. I have to go back. I have to live a normal life."

"Okay, I can not argue with that," Ultimus was starting to wonder after a year, "but why are you doing this now?"

"I have to see Dominique. I have to talk to her and tell her how I really feel. Not only that, but I feel like she is in trouble, as if her life were in danger or something."

"But how do you know where she is? What if she still thinks you are a bit odd?"

"I am not going to lose her like I lost Britania."

Ultimus was silent. It was partially Ultimus' fault that Britania had died. He held a supreme grudge against her for his entire life, and when they battled, Britania was not paying attention and got the sharp end of Zèromus' sword.

"So, I am going to end this whole live-like-a-monk lifestyle. I have to go back, be normal, and just be happy that Zèromus is gone."

"I understand."

"I just want to ask you something," Nathaniel wondered.

"Go ahead."

"Can I have your sword? The path will be far to walk, and..."

Nathaniel was holding his staff in hand, but he knew that if he were going to be serious, he would need a sword, an actual sword. Not this crude staff made of willow.

What Nathaniel was asking for was almost absurd, but Ultimus seemed to understand. In a brilliant flash of shadows and black light, the staff had become Ultimus' sword.

It was truly a work of art. It was handcrafted by hatred, designed by anguish, and forged by rage. The hum that emanated from the blade seemed to sing a song. Nathaniel remembered that hum when he had Ultimus kill the ninja bandit leader, it was singing the Hymn of Death.

With that, Nathaniel disappeared, teleporting to wherever that ruby necklace that Dominique had was.

I am coming, Dominique. I am coming for you.

I am coming...

Dominique awoke. She felt like her insides had been punched and battered. She did her best to star calm. With one blue eye, she scanned the area around her. It was dark, dank, and damp. She then remembered that the female that beat her had probably taken her here. She was standing up flat on her feet, but her arms were tied up, and the rope was tied to the ceiling. At least she could walk around, so long as the rope would let her. She was glad that these people weren't savage; otherwise they probably would have killed her.

She was cold all over. They had taken off all of her armor, but she still had the thin leather shirt and pants; although she was still decent, the leather clothes did nothing to help her against the cold. Her necklace was untouched. That is odd, they would take her armor, but not her necklace.

Where were her knights? Were they still waiting for her to get down from the mountain? Where was she anyway? She closed her eyes and tried to concentrate and save her energy.

Nathaniel, I wish you were here. Even if you could not help me, it would make me feel ten times better if I could just hear you talk to me, and it would not matter if you rambled or stuttered.

Suddenly, she felt a strong heat coming from her chest. She opened her eyes and looked down. Her necklace seemed to glow and give off heat, dispelling the chill that was pestering her. It then resonated with her heartbeat, and then she looked up. She was looking at a twenty-year-old man with red robes and a heartfelt smile. Dominique focused her eyesight, the figure was not solid, and it seemed more like a transparent ghost.

Dominique felt better at least, even if the ghost did not talk to her, looking at something that reminded her of him made her happy.

Then, the ghost seemed to move its lips, as if he were talking.

Oh! Please speak up, so she could hear him!

"Dominique..."

Was Dominique hallucinating? She could have sworn that this look-alike of Nathaniel was calling out her name.

"*I am so lonely without you. Nothing has ever been the same.*"

Dominique was touched Nathaniel was telling her how he felt about her. It was a shame that she did not like him back, but it was something Nathaniel dealt with for a long time. He lived as though he understood that there could be nothing between them, but he would not stop trying.

How sweet of him...

"Help me..."

What? What was bothering him? Was he still distraught from the death of Britania? Did he want her to help him get over his sorrow? As a friend, she would help him with anything, even if they had to talk from far away.

"Survive and search for me, I am looking for you too."

As if a hot knife had pierced butter, the ropes were severed by nothing. She wrapped her hand around her wrist, getting the soreness out. She was free, but still trapped in a cold, dank cave. She was definitely going to have trouble getting out. If someone who was armed were to find her, she would have no way of defending herself unless she relied on her fists.

She put her hand on the necklace, and the feeling of a warm hand on her shoulder made her feel better as always. With newfound confidence, she headed towards the first door she found. As soon as she got out of this place, she would rally up her knights, and go back to Ginnorum, where she would relieve the knights and search alone.

Dominique opened the door, and as soon as the door was opened, there was an opposite force that slammed the door shut. The opposite power was so great that it caused Dominique to fly back a few feet. Immediately, she recovered and got back up.

The opposite force was not a supernatural thing. In fact, it was a person who had been guarding the door. The man walked in with a smile on his face. He had a gigantic six-foot-five stature, blue armor and a crossbow that was normally used as a castle armament.

Dominique remembered this person. His name was Rubdra. He had been involved with trying to take Emy, her best friend. They would have succeeded had not Tiek, a man who liked Emy, fought off Rubdra and his brother Agnes. Rubdra was gifted with the immunity against all forms of magical spells. His brother, Agnes, was immune to all physical attacks.

"Nathaniel will not be able to recognize you when I am through with you!" Rubdra shouted. He started to run towards Dominique, but then he stopped.

"In fact, I have a better idea."

Dominique was confused. "What's that?"

"It would be a shame to kill someone as attractive as you. Perhaps you could work with me. It would be a great time we could have together." He started to chuckle a little, Dominique could tell exactly what he wanted, and she vowed to herself that he was not going to get anything.

"Keep dreaming, blue boy!" Dominique shouted.

Rubdra's face went from happy to distort within milliseconds. He ran towards Dominique and punched her in the stomach as hard as he could. Dominique's lungs had the air knocked out of them, and it was impossible for her to breathe. With a struggling gag, she fell to her knees.

Rubdra took out his crossbow and aimed for Dominique's chest.

"What a heartbreaker I am," he said, firing the crossbow.

What happened next seemed to be a phenomenon. One moment, there was a bolt flying full force at Dominique's heart. The next moment, there was a great red flash that lit up the room for a few seconds. The necklace encircled around Dominique had glowed again, and instead of providing heat, it surrounded her in a shield of some sort, protecting her from the bolt.

Rubdra was blinded, but he heard the scream of a young girl. At first, he thought he had hit her and she was crying out in pain. Instead, what was happening was that Dominique was going through some sort of weird transformation.

A gift from me to you.

Dominique's body was on fire, bursting into flames. In the beginning, Dominique began to freak out, thinking she was going to die, but the fire was doing no harm to her. In fact, she felt as if the flames were amplifying her physical strength. The necklace somehow held all of Nathaniel's fire spells, and they were all transferred to Dominique.

When the light subsided, Rubdra was looking at a woman, dressed in royal red armor, covering everything from neck to toe. Her head was the only thing unprotected. With a little style, Dominique put her hair into a ponytail with one hand, and a scary looking helmet encircled her hair. To top everything off, a red mist appeared at her hand, and then formed a sword. This weapon was polished to a mirror shine, sported serrated edges that could do more damage, and had a trail of fire following the blade whenever the sword was swished.

Rubdra's blindness had gone away, and the new look of his opponent surprised him. He quickly aimed his crossbow at Dominique and fired, only to have it deflected by her powerful armor, it did not even make a dent!

Rubdra did not give up, water bubbled from his hands and he fired a river at Dominique. She stood still, trying to show Rubdra that she was invincible, but she did not know two things. One, she certainly was not invincible. And two, water spells were her weakness. The river struck Dominique and she cried out with her teeth bared. She felt as if she was a bonfire and someone had put her out. There was sizzling sound coming from the armor, and Dominique's entire body seemed to smoke and steam.

Blinded by a short rage, Dominique charged at Rubdra with a battle cry and with her sword slicing the ground as she ran. Rubdra was ready, and he pulled out his own melee weapon, twin machetes. Dominique leaped into the air, with a trail of fire following her. Rubdra also leaped, his huge physique tunneling in the air.

Their blades met, and both figures landed on the ground. Dominique and Rubdra both looked at each other, and then Rubdra fell to the ground with a thud. There was an enormous gash that went around Rubdra's waist, the blood turning his blue armor into a sick violet. Dominique walked over to Rubdra; all the while her incredible armor was disappearing. She looked at one of Zèromus' strongest henchmen, well on the way to dying. He seemed to laugh as if he had won this fight a long time ago.

"When my master is strong enough, he is going to summon the forces of Hell and cast them upon Terra. The world will become an apocalyptic ruin. My god will it be beautiful. Nathaniel could not even fight them off if he wanted to!"

Dominique grabbed him by the scruff of his armor.

"Keep dreaming, blue boy. Nathaniel will come back, and he *will* kill his brother. There may be a Hell, and it may come to Terra, but Nathaniel *will* fight them off! I believe in him to do anything, because he is got dreams. He has goals to pursue, and he is not going to let Hell stop him!"

"How lovely, *since you are one of his goals*!" Rubdra gagged before he died.

Dominique released Rubdra's scruff and let him fall to the ground, he did not deserve any more torture. With the door no longer guarded, she left the room and escaped the mountain.

Emy walked outside from her cottage and took a great whiff of the fresh air. Today was a beautiful day. The temperature was not too hot or too cold, and there were clouds in the sky. It seemed to ring in harmony, as the sun would cause things to get hot and then the clouds would come in and cause everything to get cooler again.

She walked to her garden. Emy had spent a long time working her garden. She loved the way the colors of the flowers would clash and create a sight for sore eyes. What's more, she did all of this without the assistance of her magic powers.

Goodness, was she thirsty! Emy walked over to the

well where she got her water and looked down into it. As always, it seemed to be full of fresh water. She grabbed a ladle and dipped some water down her throat. It had a sugary taste to it, but that was how she liked it. Things could not get any better!

Then, a thought struck her mind. Where was Nathaniel? Sure, she and Nathaniel did not talk to each other much when he was around, but it would have made her day better if she had someone to enjoy this water with. Although Tiek put on the front that Nathaniel was dead and gone, he surely believed that Nathaniel was out there.

She missed him, she knew that much. Life was quieter since he left the picture, but now, she was hoping that someone would paint him back in the canvas. It was almost a flawed logical thought, but she always hoped that Dominique would get herself into some sort of danger. She knew that Nathaniel had a soft spot for Dominique, and that if she were ever in times of difficulty, Nathaniel would come for her.

Emy sat down on a comfortable chair away from the shade, letting the sun touch her tan skin. She learned a lot about Nathaniel ever since he left. She learned that he held his friends at such a high level, and that it was a serious tragedy for him if one of them were to ever disappear. If Nathaniel threw a rage like he did when Britania had passed on, imagine what he would have done had Dominique died. Could he have destroyed the world in one fell swoop?

Even if Nathaniel came just for small talk, she would feel happy in some odd way.

As if someone had answered her request, the area around her seemed to shake violently. Soon, storm clouds were everywhere; lightning appeared and struck multiple times in the same place. The wind suddenly picked up and Emy held her arm up to her face so she could brace herself.

Then a ball of electricity appeared before her feet, it almost looked like someone was bowing before her. The storm clouds dissipated, and the lightning stopped. The ball of electricity shorted out and revealed a stern looking twenty-year-old man with red robes and a gigantic sword.

Emy did not need to guess who it was. The figure did not need to guess whom he teleported to. Both people ran to each other and hugged another tightly for what seemed like forever. Sure, Nathaniel was just a friend to Emy, and Emy was just a friend to Nathaniel, but when you have not heard from someone in a year, not knowing how that person was or what they were up to, you can not help but wonder, and it sort of builds up until you see them again.

Nathaniel and Emy let go.

"I have to go, I can not stay for long," Nathaniel said, his voice was hurried, and his breathing was rapid.

"What's wrong?" Emy asked, caringly.

"Dominique is in danger. Or at least, I do not feel her in danger anymore, but I just want..."

Emy had stopped him, understanding what he meant, and happy that she was right about if Dominique were ever in trouble, he would come fore her. "I know."

"Where is she?" Nathaniel asked, seriously.

"She was looking for you."

"*What*?" Nathaniel's expression went from stern to surprise.

"Yes, in the Kazastrat Mountains. She and an expedition force of two hundred and fifty are looking for you. Boy, when Dominique sees you, she is probably going to bombard you with questions."

Nathaniel had a slight smile across his face; he had not smiled in the longest time.

Two hundred and fifty people were looking for him? That was a lot! But how many people lived in Terra? He did not remember the total population; he just knew that some people would transfer realms from Terra to Earth. He did not want to go to Earth, because he was not used to the modern technology compared to the medieval setting in this world.

It was still a good idea to go to the Kazastrat Mountains. From there, you had a good vantage point.

Nathaniel exited his train of thought and looked at Emy again. He was glad that she thought that he was still alive. He wondered how Tiek would react when he would hear Emy tell him that she found Nathaniel. He would probably go in denial again.

Nathaniel and Emy hugged one last time, and then Nathaniel disappeared quickly. When he disappeared, a shockwave knocked Emy off of her feet and she looked up to the sky in disbelief. How fast was he teleporting? The speed was easily five times faster than a normal teleportation!

Nathaniel was in the vortex. He was used to going at a speed where he could get to a faraway location within a matter of minutes. At the speed he was going, it would take him mere seconds to reach the location. Within seconds, he was at the Kazastrat Mountains. He did not think twice to walk. He jumped into the air and hovered. Nathaniel learned how to fly years ago, and now he was going to use it for once.

He lifted the sword into the air and waited for a few seconds. He was trying to find where his necklace was. After more precious seconds, the sword seemed to pull in the direction towards the east.

"Nathaniel, I swear you are whipped," Ultimus jeered.

"SHUT...UP!" That was all Nathaniel said, and Ultimus did so without arguing.

Dominique managed to get out of the cave, and she was jumping around, trying to get out of the mountain range and go back to Ginnorum with her knights. The only thing that was on her mind right now was Nathaniel, and his ghost had told her to keep looking for him. It also said that he was looking for her too.

She hoped that she had not been confused.

Oh crap! She was not paying any attention and slipped on a rock. Instinctively, she curled up into a ball to prevent her neck from breaking. Slowly, she tumbled down the mountainside, the hard rocks beating her mercilessly. It was as if the rocks were her nonliving enemy.

Oh God! This hurts! One of her arms had broken, as well as one of her legs. Then, she flipped forward and landed on her back, breaking one of the vertebrae in her back. As she landed on her backside, her tumbling stopped to a halt.

Oh, man, I can not move!

Dominique's back had taken a serious beating. One of her arms were broken, as well as one of her legs. There was no hope to her moving at all. She had to hope that her knights would find her and treat her wounds, or else she would die.

"Nathaniel...I am sorry. I tried." She spoke with difficulty.

"Do not be sorry, I am here!"

"Huh?"

Nathaniel was kneeling beside her. She was too hurt to say anything, but she did her best to smile at him. She looked into the eyes of the man who liked her, and she could not help but wonder what was on his mind at this very moment.

The young sorcerer was gentle, and put one of his arms around her back and his other arm around her legs. He was cradling her, the same way a mother cradled a newborn baby.

Nathaniel closed his eyes and concentrated. If he wanted to, he could have healed Dominique instantly. But this time, Nathaniel was purposely healing her slowly. Why? He just wanted to hold her, because it was something he always wanted to do. It was selfish, and Dominique would probably think ill towards him, but it is what he wanted.

Dominique originally had her right arm around Nathaniel's neck, with her left arm dangling helplessly. The first thing Nathaniel healed was her arm, and she immediately used it to wrap it around his neck, so she could keep herself pulled up. Now that Dominique held herself closer to him, she wanted to see his eyes, but he kept them shut on purpose. Looking at her always made him lose focus.

She started to regain the feeling in her toes, and pretty soon, her leg was totally healed. Dominique moved it around, weary that there could have been something that Nathaniel had missed. But, Nathaniel was doing a good job with the healing.

Nathaniel started to hear cracking, and his eyes wrenched open as if he heard somebody scraping their fingernails across a chalkboard. It turned out that Dominique's back was slowly healing, and that the bones were fusing together and being put back into their places. Her eyes were squinted shut and she let out some cries of discomfort. Dominique knew Nathaniel was doing his best to be gentle, but he could only heal so much without causing some sort of pain.

After about three minutes, Dominique was good as new. Nathaniel kept looking at Dominique, and she was smiling.

Then, the smile turned into a frown, and with her knee, she struck Nathaniel in the back of the head, rendering him vulnerable for a few seconds. He landed belly up and Dominique grabbed him by the scruff of his collar.

"Why did you leave like that?" she demanded, thrashing him up and down, beating him upon the ground. Nathaniel could not answer the question. He was more surprised at Dominique being mad at him than he was concerned getting hurt from being thrashed.

Dominique continued to thrash Nathaniel, and over time, there were tears in her eyes. Eventually she stopped.

"I was so worried about you! You did not leave any message, letter, note, anything! How could you have the nerve to do that? That is not like you! That is not like you at all!"

The tears were running full force and Dominique was crying. She squeezed Nathaniel, still teary eyed. Nathaniel did feel guilty, since Dominique had proven a point. She was disillusioned by the fact that if he had cared for her, he would have kept in touch with her.

"Why do I have to tell you how I am?" Nathaniel stated. "You do not share the same feelings, so why...? Why? That is my question to you."

Dominique went from sorrow to anger in a heartbeat. She tightened her grip on Nathaniel with newfound strength, nearly crushing him.

"You were wrong...very wrong...to have run off like that." Dominique lowed.

Nathaniel did not change his mind or say he was sorry. With a cross look, he forced Dominique off of him and landed her back on the ground. His voice was deadly serious.

"I had lost my best friend! It is my fault that she is dead! What good am I if I can not even protect my own friends? Can you answer that?"

Dominique was suddenly scared; Nathaniel had just raised his voice at her and used his own physical strength to knock her down.

"I do not deserve to be around. I do not even deserve to be alive today!" he recalled Dominique saving him from himself when Britania died.

He lifted his hand and out of his rage, formed a green fireball that had a sick glow coming from it. At first, Dominique thought that he was going to strike her with it, but instead he purposely shot it out into the atmosphere. When it exploded, it caused a light that shined a beautiful green, whisking away any clouds that could have been close to it, but Dominique could not help but wonder, what would have happened if Nathaniel had aimed the beam at Dominique?

"Stop it!" Dominique got up and knee bashed Nathaniel to the ground. Pretty soon, he was looking at her from the hard rock ground again.

"We need you! All of Terra needs you! Tiek, Emy, Graf, Hildegard, they *all* need you. What good are you if you are dead? Do you think that a self-inflicted death from guilt is honorable or something?" Dominique was yelling at the top of her voice.

Nathaniel was not convinced. With his arsenal of magic, he lifted Dominique away from him and stood back up. Why could he not just tell her that he came back because he really liked her? For one thing, he assumed that she already knew. He was not trying to be obvious, but he was not trying to be secret about it either.

Maybe trying to explain would not help. Instead, he did something he never did for a while.

"I am sorry."

Dominique's eyes widened. "What?"

"I am sorry I did all that. I should have told you what I was up to. I was wrong to not inform you on what I was doing. You did not deserve to be worried like that. To tell you the truth, I did not think you would worry about me."

Dominique listened whole-heartedly. Nathaniel could tell that the distorted, angry look on her face had subsided, revealing the calm, bright side of Dominique. Nathaniel then ran to Dominique and hugged her. She was still dumbstruck that Nathaniel had apologized, and it seemed to take forever for her to realize that Nathaniel had his arms around her.

After a few seconds, her arms were around him. They simply missed each other, which was all the hug went down to. It was not because of anyone liking anybody. It was simply because of two people who had not seen each other in the longest time. Nathaniel almost compared it to a class reunion. Together, they walked down the mountain and caught up on what was missed...

In Ginnorum, there was a castle where the late Queen Britania lived in, ate in, slept in, and woke up every day in. When she died, the only person to take the throne was the man who had the namesake of the city, King Ginnery. He was the first in the world to be a king, because women were labeled as higher powers than men. It felt odd to be king. To Ginnery, he felt as though he was on par with a woman in the social ladder.

Women were higher on the social ladder because Terra believed that since only women could give birth, they are the only ones capable of keeping life on Terra. It is said that a woman who lives with no children is wasting her life. The only reason why men weren't slaves to the women was because without men, there would be no life on Terra.

Nonetheless, men still had their advantages. Besides being physically stronger, they are regarded with honor if they fight on the battlefield. In Nathaniel's case, he is regarded very highly, because of his awesome magical powers. In King Ginnery's case, he was special only because he was king. According to the women, they claim that they have no special power over men, and that the men simply wanted to be gentlemen.

Even if that was the case, it still sounded ridiculous.

King Ginnery looked out the window. Slowly, a grin formed over his face...

Meanwhile, in the residential areas of Ginnorum, a young lady awoke and stretched as she yawned. The window in her room was in perfect position for the sun to gently touch her, and she looked like a goddess. At least, that is what all the men in town told her. Hildegard got out of her bed and looked out the window. As usual, there was a guy down there, trying to woo her.

Hildegard could only laugh. These men made a great effort to win her over, and a man would have to move Heaven and Hell to get her attention. Hildegard found it necessary to keep a bucket of water near the window so she could spill it down and hit anyone who kept bothering her.

Ready. Aim. Fire! The water went down and drenched the man who was holding flowers in his hand. With a sailor's cursing, he left in a huff. Life used to be so easy for Hildegard. One year ago, she was once a queen with supreme powers, but then Zèromus had taken her powers away from her. After that, Hildegard stepped down as Queen of Vicksber, and then Agnes and Rubdra attacked it. At first, Hildegard thought she was going to die without all of the perks of being Queen, but then she got used to it.

Hildegard went into her dressing room, got dressed, and walked out. Her outfit was green with a pink bow in her hair. It was almost similar to an archer's outfit, but there was no archer who would ever wear a bow in his or her hair. Hildegard was simply fashionable and knew how clothes and colors clashed and mixed.

She walked across a row of pictures, and then she stopped. She noticed the pictures of her and her friends. But then, she ran across two more pictures. One picture was of her and Nathaniel. She was smiling, but Nathaniel was not. When that picture was taken (a wizard took the picture in his mind and magically put it on a canvas), Nathaniel had gotten all wet and did not look happy. In the next picture, Nathaniel had a hearty smile while Hildegard was pulling at his ear, acting stupid.

She could not help it because she really did miss Nathaniel. She had not seen him in the longest time, and she wished that he would show up sooner or later. Back then, they used to talk a lot, but as time went on, they found each other busy and unable to hold a conversation. Sometimes, they would get fed up with each other, but then the next hour or day, they would simply forget about it.

"I wish you were here," Hildegard stated.

Suddenly, she heard a sound coming from her window. She moaned with bother. Another guy was knocking at her window. Immediately, she filled up her bucket of water and poured it down the window. Hildegard was definitely getting annoyed with all these guys trying to go out with her.

"HEY!" was the response from Hildegard's action.

That voice! She knew that voice!

She looked down the window, and there was a figure dressed in wet, red robes, and wielding a deadly looking sword. The face was something to work on, but it was a sight for sore eyes. To Hildegard, the man was a person she had not seen in a year. It was Nathaniel.

Within seconds, the door flew open and Hildegard embraced Nathaniel, disregarding his wet clothes and cold body, although her clothes would get wet too. Nathaniel was surprised from the sudden hug. He was expecting more of an angry response, the same thing he got when he came for Dominique.

"I am so glad you are here," Hildegard said.

"I am so glad you are not going to hit me like Dominique did!" Nathaniel joked sarcastically. The joke made Hildegard laugh. Nathaniel still had his sarcastic sense of humor, and now that she thought of it, he never did crack a joke in the longest time.

Nathaniel started to feel a little uneasy. All the men liked Hildegard, and now they were wondering what he did to get Hildegard to hug him. Some of them looked at him scornfully, and some of them started to get out their weapons, which of course, were torches and pitchforks.

"Hildegard, I know you have not seen me in a year, but could you please get off of me now?" Nathaniel asked, aware that he was about to cause an uproar.

"Why do not you come in for some breakfast? You look so thin! It is as if you starved yourself!"

Nathaniel coughed, as if Hildegard had figured out that he *did* starve himself. "I would love to come in..." The words surprised Hildegard. Normally, he would refuse everything she offered him, and now, he finally consented. Nathaniel really has changed in the past year. When they went inside, Hildegard managed to keep him in the house for three hours, telling him how she had all these guys hit on her. She also talked about how she lost her city and about the assassins who took it over.

Nathaniel listened to everything with wide eyes and a nodding head. He did not even dare to interrupt her. Let her keep talking, and make sure that she knows that you are listening. By doing so, Hildegard kept getting surprised every time. Nathaniel really has changed. Maybe he changed for the better, but she did was weary over what went on in that mind of his.

"I have to go now," Nathaniel muttered.

"What's wrong?" Hildegard asked.

"There's been evil things going on in Vicksber, and I must stop it before it gets worse."

"Wait a minute. You are saying it as if you can fix all the world's problems in a day. It is as if you can just go into Vicksber and then wipe it clean."

Nathaniel got up out of the chair and walked out the door.

"Because I can..." he said, as he ran out the door.

Hildegard fainted, was Nathaniel *that* powerful?

In Vicksber, there were two assassins who were sitting in the throne that used to belong to Hildegard. One of them was wearing red armor and heavy equipment. He was extremely tall and strong. This man was the late Rubdra's brother, Agnes. Agnes was a master of swordplay and had immunity to all physical attacks.

The other person was a very attractive female. Her name was Lucia. She was young, about eighteen years old, and she had blue eyes along with silky brown hair. She was dressed like an archer, which made her outfit quite revealing, but she was more proficient in spell work. Lucia was not as strong as most spell warriors, but she had the uncanny ability to make her body grow three times her size, making her fifteen feet high.

Agnes could not help but remember back to how he took the city over. He and his brother, along with Lucia, attacked people, destroyed buildings, and overtook the guards that were supposed to protect the small town. The guards did not even put up much of a fight. Riots happened every day; people had died, got hurt, or were treated unfairly.

He received the word that his brother had died, and he swore that he would kill the ungrateful wretch who did this. When he heard that the killer was a woman, he could not help but feel ashamed. Here, his brother was an extremely powerful archer who died to a woman with glowing red armor.

If that were the case, he would not have to worry. He was immune to all physical attacks done to him. Let them all come, he thought, because no one could take over and liberate this city!

All of a sudden, the beautifully crafted doors had crumbled into a thousand pieces. Someone was attacking! Immediately, he stood up with his sword in hand. The person walking closer to him was someone that he recognized. The brown hair, the red robes, and the green light emanating from the figure told him that this was Nathaniel.

Agnes started to worry. The last time he and Nathaniel fought, Nathaniel pretty much had him beat. How did he get past all of the guards that were guarding the castle? Did Nathaniel take them all out that quickly?

"Oh, Agnes, there's something you need to know," Nathaniel stated.

"What's that?" Agnes shouted, ready to strike.

"I am taking back this city, and I am going to dispose of you."

The words themselves brought fear to Agnes. This young man was just telling the hulking knight that he would die here, and he actually believed it!

"Lucia! Attack!" Agnes roared.

Lucia grinned with a smirk, and charged at Nathaniel full force. When Nathaniel and Dominique were walking down the mountain, she was talking about how a girl came and knocked her out. The descriptions matched perfectly. Lucia was the one who attacked Dominique at the Kazastrat Mountains.

But yet, there was something about Lucia that kept Nathaniel's judgment at bay. Was she really evil, or was she under some sort of possession?

Lucia threw a punch at Nathaniel, but a green spot came from nowhere and protected the wizard. She threw all sorts of fancy punches and kicks, along with some somersaults, but Nathaniel's shield was impregnable. With a flick of Nathaniel's fingers, Lucia was knocked back.

The archer quickly readied herself and took a battle stance. This time, she was taking in all the power she could absorb. Nathaniel could feel huge amounts of energy flowing around him and all of it was heading towards Lucia. After about fifteen seconds, Lucia fell to one knee and moaned. This was a lot of energy to handle. Nathaniel was unsure whether or not he could do what she was trying to do.

Then, the sound of squishing muscles and crunching bones could be heard. Lucia was using all of her magical power to sprout three times her normal size. Slowly, her body grew foot by foot, towering over Nathaniel. Her clothes grew along with the change, but her footwear had ripped apart. Nathaniel could see the muscles move around in Lucia's arms, legs, feet, and stomach. He was certain that her physical strength had just been amplified by ten times the normal power.

Lucia then aimed a punch at Nathaniel, and the shield came to protect him again. This time, however, the shield looked like a green sphere and it had shattered like glass. Nathaniel lost his shield after one punch from Lucia.

Nathaniel was impressed, but he knew that she could never beat him. With one twitch, Nathaniel became Ultimus, and the grin on his face was sinister. Dramatically, he spun around and punched Lucia once, square in the stomach. Lucia lost her breath, and her mouth was wrenched open with the loss of air. She tried her hardest to breathe, but Ultimus had just beaten her in her awesome fifteen feet stature with one single punch.

Just as slowly as her body grew into a tremendous size, Lucia started to shrink back to normal. Instead of squishing and crunching, there was the sound of fusing and rushing water. Nathaniel looked at Lucia again and could see the muscles shrinking, contracting, and going back to normal. He walked by the archer as she was going back into the weak human she was.

Ultimus stared at Agnes. Agnes knew his time was coming soon, and he bowed to him, ready to die.

"Kill him," Nathaniel's voice was heard. "Kill him quickly."

"With pleasure!"

Ultimus simply snapped his fingers. He performed no magical spell whatsoever, but Agnes suffered a heart attack and died on the spot. Being scared like that can do something to you, and it was understandable why Agnes died like that.

Seconds after his death, Lucia started to quiver and shake violently. She had her hands up to her forehead, and smoke was escaping her. She was growing three times her size, and then suddenly shrinking. It looked like there was a connection between Agnes' death and her. Light escaped from Ultimus and became Nathaniel again, and he walked towards Lucia.

As he approached her, he noticed that she had a Z on her forehead. Now he understood why. Anyone with a Z on their forehead signified that they were property of Zèromus. Agnes and Rubdra both had one, so did a small number of soldiers. Lucia was probably one of many in Zèromus' harem of women, and he was probably calling her back to the castle. One could only guess what he would want. Nathaniel made a conjecture that Lucia was going through anguish and suffering as she was trying to defy Zèromus' orders. She really was going through the pain in her mind.

Nathaniel would not have it. He placed his hand on Lucia's forehead and she instantaneously calmed down. All the feelings of hatred, darkness, malice, and evil simply left her. She suddenly felt at peace, as she was filled with gentleness and a calming sensation flowing through her.

"That Z isn't good for you, especially on a face as pretty as yours. Close your eyes."

Nathaniel pressed hard on Lucia's forehead, and with a slow, individual swipe, the Z was wiped away like dust on the wood.

Nathaniel released his grip and backed away from Lucia. Before, there was darkness in her eyes, but then it disappeared along with the Z. Her eyes were truly bright before Zèromus had taken her over. It was sad; no one deserved to be deprived of his or her looks. Nathaniel himself was not attractive, and he would not do anything to make himself look any worse.

Lucia looked at Nathaniel. She did not know him, but she certainly hoped that they could get to know each other. After all, he had just freed her from servitude of an evil person. She ran up to him and hugged him, with tears running down her face.

"I do not know you, but thank you. Thank you, thank you, and thank you," she cried.

"I do not know you, but you are welcome. You are welcome, you are welcome, and you are welcome," Nathaniel replied sarcastically.

"Who are you, and what kind of powers do you have?" she asked, suddenly talkative and questioning him.

"I can not answer all of your questions. But take my hand, and I will take you to my friends, and you can talk to them. There's no place for you here."

Lucia did so immediately. Nathaniel hesitated for a moment. He knew he liked Dominique, but she never did return his feelings. But then again, if he started liking someone else, then all the time he invested in Dominique would be all for naught. Could he really let go of a girl he liked for all these years?

"Do it!" Ultimus screamed.

"Be quiet," Nathaniel replied.

"I beg your pardon?" Lucia asked, who could not hear Ultimus.

"Nothing, let's go."

Lucia's soft hands clasped with Nathaniel's soft hands and they were off to Ginnorum. Within seconds, they were in Hildegard's house. Hildegard was surprised at first, but then she suddenly calmed down when she found out that it was Nathaniel. When she saw Lucia, she thought Nathaniel had picked up a girlfriend.

"Ooooh..."

"NO! Lucia, this is Hildegard. Hildegard, this is Lucia. I need to go talk to the King, so you two behave yourselves, alright?"

He did not wait for a reply, he teleported to the castle.

"I need to speak to the King," Nathaniel said to Graf.

Graf was almost happy to see him, but he was sarcastic to say something. "Nice to see you too, Nathaniel."

Nathaniel lowered his head. "I am sorry, but I feel like I am being rushed."

"Rushed?"

"Yeah, I feel like my life is a book and that I have only eleven pages left."

Graf laughed. "Why only eleven? Alright, well, the King wanted to see you anyway."

Nathaniel and Graf bid each other good day, and he walked inside the castle. As always, Graf enchanted the door so that when Nathaniel walked in it, he would be standing next to the King. He bowed down to King Ginnery.

"It is been a while, Nathaniel," Ginnery said with a deep voice.

"Huh? But this is my first time seeing you," Nathaniel said, confused.

"Right. So, how are you?"

"I have returned from my disappearance, and I liberated Vicksber for you."

"Yes, you have saved us years of work. Unfortunately, you have caused me a lifetime of trouble."

Nathaniel was confused once more. "What are you talking about?"

Ginnery then clenched his fists, and Nathaniel was suddenly surprised as he was lifted off his feet. "Look past these eyes and see your enemy."

Nathaniel did not want to accept it, but every feeling in his soul told him that Ginnery was not even real. It was someone else. It was someone that he did not want to remember, or even think about. Unfortunately, it was the man that Nathaniel swore to kill. The man impersonating the fake King Ginnery was none other than Zèromus in disguise.

But now, Nathaniel could not do anything because Zèromus incapacitated him.

"I am very glad to have escaped the coffin that you sealed me in. While I was gone, I took the time to look at the playing field to see what I am up against. Pretty soon, I will unleash a Hell on Terra, and you could not even take them on, even with the assistance of Ultimus."

Ultimus growled.

"At any rate, I have already won!" he snapped his fingers, and Nathaniel looked in horror as he saw Emy, Dominique, Hildegard, and Lucia all stood in front of him, scared and confused over what was going on. They were all wearing some sort of pink silk outfits. Nathaniel wondered in horror what the outfits were for.

"I managed to have the guards of the city imprison them. The only person who escaped was that Elfin man Tiek."

"Help us!" Dominique cried out, her hand reaching out for him.

"Dominique!" Nathaniel tried to move, but Zèromus stopped him. Then, Zèromus lifted Nathaniel even further into the air and with invisible arms, started to beat Nathaniel senselessly. With a fling, Nathaniel flew across the air and landed at the women's feet. Emy and Lucia helped him up and while Dominique used a weak healing spell to treat the wounds. She still had the necklace around her neck. Nathaniel smiled at her and morphed into Ultimus. This time, he charged at Zèromus and launched every attack, physical and magical, at him. Zèromus was not going to go down. He had dodged every attack and threw a gigantic icicle at him, throwing Nathaniel back at the women.

Ultimus turned back into Nathaniel. It was pointless, even with all of Ultimus' powers; they could not even get a hit on the bad guy. Dominique kneeled down on one knee and looked down upon the man who she regarded as her hero.

Zèromus then grabbed Dominique and placed his hands on her forehead. After a few seconds, a Z was on her forehead, and her facial expressions suddenly changed.

"Kill him," Zèromus said to her.

Dominique's pink harem outfit suddenly morphed into the fiery knight's outfit. With a charge, she attacked Nathaniel. At first, Nathaniel did not think that she would attack him, but she was under Zèromus' control now. Zèromus was amused as he watched Dominique kick Nathaniel's rear end. He would have fought back, but this was Dominique, and he would not dare raise a finger against her.

"Aww, does Britania's death still hold you back?" Zèromus jeered.

Nathaniel suddenly went mad and struck Dominique in the chest. The hit knocked her back a few feet and took off the Z from her forehead.

He then looked at Zèromus with all forms of hatred.

He killed Britania and Lilium.

He hurt Dominique.

He took all those sorceress' powers against their will.

He ruined his life.

And now, Nathaniel was going to make him pay for all of the wrong things he did. He did not care if he died killing Zèromus. He only wanted two things. He wanted to rid the world of this demented killer, and he wanted to protect Dominique with everything he had. He would give up everything for her, even his own life.

After all, he did love Dominique...

"AHHHHH...!" Nathaniel and Ultimus yelled together as a white light exploded from within him. The light was so luminous that it would have caused the blind to see and the sighted to become blind. It even caused the walls of the castle to tumble and the ceiling to explode. The people outside the castle, completely oblivious to who Zèromus even was, were immediately blinded by the huge amounts of light coming from what was supposed to be the castle. Someone in space could have sworn they had seen a flash of light from the ground.

Zèromus had his eyes shielded from the great explosion. Was there something to the fifth element that he did not know about? What the heck was Nathaniel doing?

The light cleared completely except for the glow that was coming from where Nathaniel stood. Zèromus looked at Nathaniel and could see a figure similar to Nathaniel. His eyes were white, his hair was white, his robes had become royal bright armor, and there were wings that had sprouted from his back. The sword that Nathaniel had was no longer called the Hymn of Death. Rather, it was the Hymn of Heaven. Songs and glorious choirs could be heard. Out of all those voices, Britania's could be heard.

"*And now...*" Nathaniel's voice could be heard, like it was echoing. "*You will die for all the sins you have ever committed.*"

Zèromus heard every word, but he was still defiant.

"You have nerve telling me what you will do, considering I am the devil!"

Zèromus released all of his magical powers and, in a long demonic silence, became a gigantic demon-like creature. The sky had turned blood red, and creatures were popping out of the ground. There were currents of evil creatures from the air. Hell had come to ravage Terra, and Zèromus would be the one leading it with a cruel and unusual shaped fist.

Nathaniel looked up, worried of what would come, and then he walked to Dominique and kneeled to her.

"*No matter what happens, even if I am swallowed up by this Hell that has come to destroy this world, I will always love you. Without you, I could not have done this. Without you, I have no hope to live and no hope to live for.*"

Nathaniel flew into the air and after some time, armies of soldiers were at his command. Some of them were Ginnorum's soldiers. Some of them were Vicksber's soldiers. Some were from Kazastrat and

Parlona, while some were heavenly soldiers created by Nathaniel's newfound power. Nathaniel even summoned his dog, Pooch, to help.

"Today we fight...for Terra!"

There was a roar. And with a mighty thunderclap, the standing army charged at the forces of Hell...

It was a terrible fight. Nathaniel would kill everything left and right easily. The soldiers did their best. Their main job was simply for defense and not for offense. The forces of Hell weren't bothering with Nathaniel, they only wanted to kill normal humans and destroy tall buildings. Red lightning had struck the ground multiple times, and Terra was shaking like there were earthquakes everywhere.

Tiek had shown up and was able to hold his own. Emy had managed to wear her normal outfit and shot spells of her own. Unfortunately, the only thing they could do was slow down the forces. The only people capable of taking down the demonic creatures were the heavenly soldiers and Nathaniel. Lucia fought alongside Nathaniel, but Nathaniel had to keep an eye on Lucia, because he was worried that she would note able to hold her own.

Dominique, however, was still standing still. She was still heartfelt. Nathaniel had just told her that he had loved her. And he meant it, regardless of what she felt about him.

"Take that!" Nathaniel yelled as he fired a ball of light at a demon. Demons were the strongest of all the forces of Hell. It took ten knights just to slow one down. As the creatures died, a spirit would float freely and go to Nathaniel. As the spirits accumulated, there was a growing white light glowing from Nathaniel's right arm.

The demon was destroyed, and Nathaniel's arm

shined and resonated. Instantly, his arm turned into some sort of cannon. What was this? Nathaniel could feel massive energy coming from it.

Well, why not use it?

Nathaniel flew into the air and fired the cannon. The force of its shooting knocked Nathaniel backward, but the moment it touched the ground, there was a gigantic explosion. Any demonic creature touching this white light had died. What's more, the area that was hit had a beautiful setting. It was as if Hell had never touched it. A tree that was standing there, chopped down by the enemies, was standing up beautifully. The grass that was once scorched was a beautiful green.

Did Nathaniel's cannon destroy the evil and restore what was once good?

The city was overrun. The undead and evil were coming from the ground and attacking the villagers. Nathaniel quickly made short work of them, and the town looked as beautiful as it ever did on a sunny day. What's more, when any area was restored, the forces of Hell could not touch it again. It was as if God had put a "No Devil" sign on a protected area.

Nathaniel looked up, and he could see Zèromus, taller than a giant, overlooking everything. Using most of his power, he shot a gigantic beam of pure energy at Zèromus. There was an explosion, and everything turned back to normal.

Zèromus, in his human state, was lying on the ground, cursing to himself. How come he did not have a cannon? It was not fair, because no matter how hard he tried, Nathaniel seemed to have him stomped. Slowly, he got up and the moment he did, he was staring at Nathaniel in his angel form.

"*I have been waiting for this!*" Nathaniel howled in triumph.

"Really? I see it quite differently!" Zèromus crowed.

He charged up for a massive thunder attack. Nathaniel was alert. Even though he was easily much stronger than Zèromus, a strong attack could knock him out of his angelic form, and he would not have a chance against his twin brother in his human state.

Then, Lucia jumped in front of Nathaniel.

"*Lucia?*" Nathaniel asked, confused.

Lucia stretched herself out as she grew into her fifteen-foot stature again. She was willing to take the hit and save Nathaniel from what could have happened.

Zèromus, drunk with power and blinded by rage, fired every lightning bolt he had. Lucia was taking the full brunt of the attack. At first, she did not feel anything because she had extra energy from her transformation. Unfortunately, it only protected her for so long. Within seconds, her body had burst into flames and there was electricity everywhere. She was crying out in pain as the lightning paid her neither heed nor mercy. Eventually, Zèromus stopped the current and Lucia fell to the ground, shrinking back to her normal size.

Nathaniel immediately ran to her and held her up.

"*You do not even know me, and yet you would jump in to protect me?*"

"I am just returning the favor," Lucia answered, and passed out. Nathaniel looked at the man that was his twin brother. He did not think for a second, but he knew what he wanted to do.

Without hesitation, the wind rushed as Nathaniel charged at Zèromus with his sword in hand.

Dominique finally got herself together, and she headed towards Emy and Tiek, who were exhausted from the major battles.

"Is everyone alright?" she asked.

Emy coughed out some smoke, but then she said, "I am fine, but I am wondering what made you freeze up like that while we were fighting."

"Apparently, you did not hear what he said to me before he fought Zèromus."

Emy laughed. "Oh, I heard everything!"

Tiek remarked, "Me too. I can not see how he can still like you after all this time. It is almost as if the more you ignore him, the more he wants you to be with him."

Dominique threw her hands up in the air and said, "Fine, so you heard it!"

"What holds you back?" Hildegard asked, coming into the picture.

Dominique then sat down and wrapped her arms around her knees. She felt like everyone was pressuring her.

"I do not like him because he *is* Nathaniel."

Emy was confused. "Wait a second; you do not like him because he is what he is?"

"Exactly."

Emy turned around and buried her face in her hand. She could not help but wonder how Nathaniel would take it if he had heard what she just heard.

By the way, where *was* Nathaniel?

Graf came running to Dominique and Tiek. He was out of breath, and had his hands on his knees.

"What's wrong?" Tiek asked him.

"It is Nathaniel, he is fighting someone!" Graf said, struggling to get the words out.

"Are you okay?" Dominique asked him.

"No." Graf fell to the ground, and they could see the arrows engraved in his back. Some of Zèromus' human soldiers were still alive and fighting for him.

Graf had sacrificed his life to warn the group that someone was in trouble.

Hildegard picked up Graf. "I do not have any magical powers, and so I am of no use to you all. I will get this man to his family. You three go on and help Nathaniel in any way."

Tiek loaded his quiver with flaming arrows, Emy brandished her battle staff, and Dominique donned the fiery knight outfit. Together, they ran to the opposite direction that Graf was running in hopes of assisting Nathaniel.

Meanwhile, Nathaniel and Zèromus were having a swordfight to the death. Nathaniel's Hymn of Heaven did not even scratch the blade of Zèromus' sword, which was called "Hell's Edge."

Nathaniel did a horizontal swipe, and it was immediately parried by Zèromus' hulking sword. This fight seemed to go on forever. Zèromus then jumped into the air and brought down a vertical slash upon Nathaniel, but he raised his hands and grabbed the blade.

Impossible! How could he have done that?

Nathaniel, with his grip on the blade, flung his twin brother across the battlefield. Blood was dripping from his hands, but the pain never entered his mind. What was pain to Nathaniel? What was anguish of the mind? What was the anger that kept him strong in times of need?

Zèromus got up. He was exhausted, but he was not about to give up. Wow, Nathaniel has become really powerful! His twin brother was going to stop at nothing to kill him this time.

Nathaniel was about to speed for Zèromus, but then he was stopped.

"Let me out!" Ultimus yelled.

"*What?*"

"Let me out! Now that you have the final power unlocked, I can be free and we can both team up on Zèromus. After all, he did kill my sister."

"*Good point...*" Nathaniel agreed.

Nathaniel stretched out and focused some of his energy. After a quick bright flash, he was looking at an elf. The elf looked very similar to Nathaniel. He had brown hair, greenish eyes, and a tall stature. He almost looked like Lilium in a way. After all, they were brother and sister.

"It feels good to move around freely again," Ultimus said. His deep voice was gone and back to the way he normally spoke all those years ago.

"*Right, now let's take him!*" Nathaniel roared, and sped off to Zèromus with Ultimus at his side.

Zèromus was ready. This time, there were two people heading toward him.

"Crap," he said to himself. Two people were going to make his life a lot harder. He looked around, and could see that he still had some of his forces intact. Heck, he could have them help him in this battle so his life could be a little easier.

"Hey! Get over here and help me out!"

Zèromus still had a force of about one hundred men. Most of them were archers, but whoever weren't archers could easily pick up a fallen sword and throw it.

Nathaniel and Ultimus both came to Zèromus and the squared off. Nathaniel was weakened only by a slight margin when he released Ultimus, but at least he had a helper to assist him in the fight. However, after a few minutes, both Nathaniel and Ultimus were dodging left and right to avoid arrows and javelins being hurled at them.

They took to the air and fought there. Being in the air caused the rules of sword fighting to change drastically, particularly because when you are in the air, you can perform vertical slashes and not have an end until you hit the ground. It is very hard to stop yourself, especially when you miss a vertical slash. What's more, when you miss, you are open to everything.

Even though the three were fighting in the air, the arrows and javelins did not stop flying. Zèromus was using this opportunity to heal and rest up. If he had enough time, he could perform one last spell...

Dominique, Emy, and Tiek had rushed to the battlefield. They were using the terrain to keep themselves hidden. Dominique looked up and could see Nathaniel and Zèromus, but who was the third figure that was hovering above the ground? Could that have been Ultimus? She was not quite sure, she only cared that Nathaniel was still alive.

The three popped their heads over the covering, and they could see one hundred men. All of them were firing their arrows and any projectiles that they picked up. Some of them even had the audacity to pick up rocks and throw them. One of the rocks managed to get in Nathaniel's way, distracting him and causing him to get punched by Zèromus.

Tiek was enraged. He loaded three arrows in his bow and fired. He did not care how much arrows he had, Emy could always make more for him. Emy stood out and fired lightning bolts at the opponents. After about fifteen men had been killed, they began to realize that they were being attacked from the ground. Once they caught sight of Emy and Tiek, they shifted to them.

Emy was about to duck for cover, but then an arrow struck her in the arm. She fell over the covering. She was safe, but hurt. Dominique used slight healing spells to get the sting out of her arm. Other than that, Emy would have difficulty trying to move her left arm.

Dominique then burst out of the covering. She was still wearing her red armor. The archers caught sight of her and fired arrow after arrow on her, but the arrows did hardly anything to her armor. She leaped into the air and brought her sword upon the ground, causing everything around her to explode, killing about twenty men.

Tiek was next. He fired like an arbalest and racked up five kills. He then started throwing fireballs everywhere, but the enemies were smart to duck, killing only two men.

Forty-two men had been dispatched of, leaving fifty-eight.

Zèromus was still holding off Nathaniel and Ultimus, and he noticed that the amount of arrows and javelins protecting him had dwindled by half. He looked down and could see three figures causing trouble. How could three people take out nearly half of his forces? Did he train his men for naught?

Emy was able to move her arm, and she stepped over the covering to fire more spells at Zèromus' henchmen. However, when she stepped over the covering, she was staring at Zèromus right in the face. Emy was unable to move, the fear stopped her from being able to take any action. Tiek noticed Zèromus and immediately stepped in to protect her. Unfortunately, Zèromus had eye lasers and, with one shot, paralyzed Tiek.

Dominique had seen that Emy was in trouble, and she ran to her aid. Zèromus drew out his thick sword and parried attacks with Dominique. Zèromus was more of a slow but powerful attacker. Dominique's attacks were quicker, but did not deal as much power. She aimed a vertical attack and Zèromus stepped aside, leaving her open. He put his hands on her forehead and a Z appeared. Again, Dominique was under the evil sorcerer's control. He also approached Emy and touched her forehead with his finger, and then he ran it down her neck. Emy, although scared, tried to shake off Zèromus with her battle staff. The moment she resisted, a Z appeared on her forehead, and she lost control of herself.

"Assist the woman in blonde hair and take down Nathaniel!"

"Yes, master," Emy responded. Together, she and Dominique headed towards Nathaniel and Ultimus, who had finished off the remainder of Zèromus' henchmen.

Nathaniel decided to attack Emy, and Ultimus would handle Dominique. Ultimus raised his Hymn of Death at Dominique and understood why Nathaniel would never attack her. Nathaniel would never raise a finger towards Dominique, even if she wanted to kill him.

Emy was easily weaker than Nathaniel, but because she was under control of someone else, it seemed like her power had no limits. She lifted her hands and charged a massive fireball. Nathaniel raised a finger but nothing seemed to happen. Emy then threw the fireball like a softball at Nathaniel, but the moment it got within two feet of him, it disappeared as if it were doused with water.

Dominique utilized her quick attacks at Ultimus, but he was an elf, and a master of footwork. Ultimus parried an attack and then spun around and kicked Dominique square in the chest.

Nathaniel was fighting Emy, but the moment he heard a woman groan, he could not help but look for Dominique. Sure, she was an enemy now because she was under control, but he could not help but wonder and care.

That one-second of caring left him open, and Emy took that opportunity to launch a gravitational spell at Nathaniel. Gravitational spells were extremely powerful, because it used gravity to attack its opponents. It could never kill anyone, but it always took off three-quarters of a person's health.

The attack put Nathaniel on his knees. It would not matter how strong he was, a gravitational spell would always bring you major pain and suffering. He was almost about to fall unconscious.

Do not give up, Nathaniel!

Who was that?

Do not let my death hinder you. I am always looking down upon you with a smile.

Britania?

I believe in you. You have liked Dominique for the longest time. If you were going to die, at least you would die protecting her.

I can do it...

That is the spirit!

"*Thanks, Britania,*" Nathaniel said to himself. Emy had stopped when she heard the words and then she looked around. Who was he talking to?

Nathaniel started to walk to Emy, and she started to be afraid. She fired another gravitational spell at him, and it took off three-quarters of his already quarter-of-a-tank health, but he just kept on walking.

Emy then fired lightning bolts and fireballs at him, but he continued to walk towards her. Was he invincible?

Nathaniel stopped walking when he approached Emy, and then he wrapped his arms around her. Instantly, the Z on Emy's forehead was destroyed and out of sight. She began to feel the gentle energy that ruminated from Nathaniel.

"*I love you, Dominique,*" he said, and then he fell to the ground, and his angel form disappeared, revealing Nathaniel in his red robes and normal attire.

Emy almost had a tear running down her face. He was probably so hurt after all of those spells that he started to see things differently. In this case, Nathaniel thought that Emy was Dominique. What's more, she was just told by Dominique that she would never like him back that way. And yet, he still carried on. Emy could not help but sympathize for Nathaniel's bleeding heart.

Dominique was still fighting Ultimus, but she was beginning to tire out. Ultimus managed to grab one of her arms and pin her down on the ground. He was trying to put his hand on her forehead to get the Z off, but Dominique put up the fight of her life. She even screamed out of frustration and desperation.

Emy was trying to wake up Nathaniel, but it was tough. After Emy fired the first gravitational spell, he lost seventy percent of his health, and when he was hit again, he was dwindled down to about six percent of health left. He was almost on the verge of dying.

However, the moment Dominique's scream reached Nathaniel's ears, it seemed like Nathaniel's health had went to one hundred and fifty percent. With a gigantic burst of light, he turned into the angel form and sped for Dominique. He was blinded by rage, so he could not notice Ultimus. The moment Nathaniel punched Ultimus out of the way; he understood everything and felt like an idiot.

Dominique was freed, and she looked at Nathaniel, but that was all they did. They did not hug, talk, or anything. It looked like they were having some sort of staring contest.

They both looked to Dominique's right and could see Zèromus charging up for his final spell.

It all happened in a split second. Nathaniel had pushed Dominique out of the way; Zèromus fired a high-speed projectile that looked like a black ball. Nathaniel was hit and death finally had a grip on him. Before Nathaniel yielded to the darkness, he raised his hand and was about to fire all of his energy.

Could you ever forgive yourself? The voice of Lilium rang in his mind.

If I could save Dominique from death, that is all I want. I will not forgive myself for killing my own brother, but I will not forgive myself if he is left to live either.

Nathaniel fired all of his power at Zèromus, and then he fell to the ground and closed his eyes.

Zèromus was struck by a bright ball of light, seconds after Nathaniel was struck. Over time, beams and trickles of red, green, and blue light escaped him and he disappeared like an apparition or a ghost would. When every trace of his body was gone, there was an explosion, and then the daytime began to be veiled with dark clouds.

It began to rain.

Emy reached out her hands and felt the water touch her arms, how long had it been since it last rained?

Tiek looked up, realizing that rain was a once-in-a-lifetime opportunity.

Dominique got up and felt the rain too. Nathaniel had just saved her from death. Then, she looked around. Where did Nathaniel go?

Then she looked down, and there was a big difference between rain and tears. Nathaniel was lying on the ground, lifeless, emotionless, and dead. She knelt down and with her left arm raised his upper body. It gave the appearance that she was cradling him the same way he cradled her when she slipped off the mountainside.

Hildegard and Lucia approached too, but they did not have to be told about what had happened. Nathaniel had died and killed Zèromus before passing on.

Dominique's grip on the dead body tightened, and her face buried itself into Nathaniel's shoulder. The thunder started to roll, and Dominique began to cry out in pain and sorrow.

This was the second time that Nathaniel had left her without being able to say good-bye. This time though, Dominique could not go out and search for him. Nathaniel was not going to show up again. This was permanent. He was gone for good, and he was never going to come back.

"No..." Dominique cried. "No, please do not go. I do not want you to go. I want you here..."

Emy, who also had a tear running down her face, walked up to her. "He is gone. You have to let go of him."

"NO!" Dominique kept a firm grip on Nathaniel, and then she whispered to him, "Why do I feel your hand on my shoulder?"

Tiek stepped in. "Dominique, we have to go. Lightning will start and you will be hit."

"I am not going."

Tiek was dumbstruck, and then angry. "Dominique, he is dead!"

"Go. I will join you soon," Dominique responded.

Tiek, Emy, Lucia, and Hildegard had all left. Tiek had looked at Nathaniel one last time before leaving, and then looked at Dominique. Nathaniel sacrificed his life for her, how noble.

Dominique and Nathaniel were alone. Well, Dominique was alone at least. She looked at the man that was nothing but kind to her, and liked her no matter how much she did not like him. The man that helped her with her classes, attended her graduation, and saved her from death two different times. Now, he was gone, unable to be brought back.

Whatever held her back had melted, and even though he could not hear her, she said everything that was on her mind.

"Nathaniel..."

Hesitation stopped her, but there was no point in being afraid. Lightning started to hit the ground.

"I am sorry that I took you for granted. I should have treated your heart with more respect. I need you here with me, but that can never happen. I am so glad that you can only die once, because my heart could only take this sadness once.

"If I could do anything to bring you back, I would do it in a heartbeat."

Dominique could feel that hand on her shoulder. She closed her eyes and held Nathaniel close to her. She started to run her hands through his hair, like she was trying to make him comfortable. Every time she stroked his face or touched his hair, she only got worse and worse. She was told by a lot of rumors that Nathaniel's hair was ugly and ratty, but she never really believed that. Here, her hands were stroking his hair, and by golly, it was as soft as goose down.

She could not help but wonder. She never knew

what she had until it was gone. Dominique was sure that Nathaniel would not think that she took him for granted, but she could not convince herself that Nathaniel was not disappointed in the fact that Dominique just simply did not like him, not like that.

What did she ever do that made him like her? All of her friends always asked him the same question as a kid, and the answers were always the same. "She was nice to me."

Dominique put her hand on the necklace that Nathaniel had given her a long time ago. She realized then that she did not need it anymore. She unclipped it and put in Nathaniel's hand and squeezed his hand shut. Once it was shut, she lifted it up to her mouth and she kissed his hand. With more tears, she laid Nathaniel's hand down on his chest. The rain amplified. She stood up and walked away, fighting off every urge to look back at Nathaniel.

When the weather cleared and the people came back to look at their hero, Nathaniel was gone. They could tell that he had been dragged, but the paths were split, and the people gave up their search after a while.

A few years passed. Emy, Tiek, Hildegard, and Lucia, all were about twenty-one years old. Emy and Tiek were married and had two children of their own.

Hildegard secured her position as Queen of Vicksber again, and she was still single, trying to hold off all the men that kept asking for her hand in marriage. They claimed that she just kept getting prettier every day.

Lucia, although not very well mentioned, was last heard from working on a new weapon called. "The Gun."

Ultimus went back and rebuilt his village of Ab'Dornum, where he became the leader of the elves.

As for Dominique, she lived a secluded life in a cottage up in the Kazastrat Mountains, where she trained hard every day and hunted gigantic rock solid golems for a living. She went out with a few men, but she could not help but think of Nathaniel throughout the years.

She never forgot all of the good times she and Nathaniel shared together, whether it was when they were kids, teenagers, and young adults. She managed to convince herself one time that she actually did love him, but that was quickly dispelled when she realized from that viewpoint that Nathaniel had been dead.

Still though, she felt proud of herself that she managed to keep the relationship with Nathaniel strictly as friends. Dominique knew that two lovers could keep secrets from each other, but friends could tell friends anything. Nathaniel loved Dominique as a friend so much that he was able to comfortably say that he loved her.

One day, there was a knock at her door. At first, she was surprised.

Who in their right mind would come to visit her?

She stopped sharpening her sword and walked over to the door. At first, she was wondering if it was a man or someone who needed help with getting rid of a monster. Then, she wondered if it was Emy, Tiek, or someone who could pay her a visit.

She opened the door and looked up. At first, she could have believed that she was going insane. Then, she could have thought that she had fallen asleep and was dreaming, although she was perfectly sane.

In either case, she was staring at a man with a broad smile on his face, wearing red robes and holding a staff made of willow.

Dominique Delacroix and Nathaniel Leonhart embraced each other.

The moment endured...until their next adventure!

The End...